DOMES

John Pascal

The Revelation Trilogy, Part Two

The story of The Bee continues.

DOMES, second edition,
March, 2022

Bible quotations are from “The New International Version”, 1984, Zondervan.

DEDICATION

The Revelation Trilogy is lovingly dedicated to my Junior High science teacher, Mr. J.F. Main, who inspired me to discover and enjoy the reality of this world, and to the Holy Spirit who delights in showing me there is so much more reality beyond our senses.

THE QDT: 2247

Officer Rollins grabbed his prisoner's steel neck collar and smashed his head against the wall. The pleasure of the delivered blow oozed out from the corner of his smirk. "All right, Sammy boy, so you're in charge of the Director's security, huh? Let's hear about why you're trying so hard to *protect* everyone. And just where is Director Justin?"

Samuel 421 spit out the blood in his mouth, wriggled around in his arm shackles, and leaned against the wall. "Because it's my *job* of course, as is following the law. Making sure Professor Main got back to 1986? That was Justin's job—his obligation."

The Swat Chief reached for Samuel's ear and turned his face toward him. "They can't hide in this building forever, Sammy. It's surrounded."

"No need, they're already gone--left in Bee 76."

Rollins sucked in a deep breath. "Damn! So you can launch a full sized Bee from the Drone Bay?" He glowered down at Samuel who returned a quiet, defiant gaze. "So of *course* you were in on it." He decided Sammy needed a whack in the stomach. "Planned! You all had it planned. You're just lucky I need your brain intact for a memory scan."

Something occurred to the hulking police soldier, and he bent down to Samuel's face. "Our four man Swat Team, the ones who were in the arrival bay…" He coughed. "OK, where are you hiding *them*?"

Samuel grinned. "They're in the second floor break room with the district Magistrate—being interrogated."

Rollins laughed and released his hold. "So you thought *you'd* do the arresting, huh? Sorry, but you won't be available to press charges." He shoved his prisoner toward another officer with a chuckle, and leaned into his shoulder mike: "You got all the QDT department heads outside? Good. Send 'em in."

Six people in leg irons, arms cuffed behind their backs, shuffled in, each one with a guard. "*All* of you are under arrest in the name of Aten for treason and blasphemy, not to mention obstruction of justice."

Rollins strode toward a diminutive young woman. With a meaty hand he grabbed the straight black hair on the back of her head and jerked her face upward. "*This* is the one I want—the Computer Chief. We'll add 'assault on police officers' to *your* charge." He sneered and glanced around at his helpers. "She was with the Director when the Bee arrived." He gave her head a shake. "Weren't you?"

Anna's head was bent backward in his grip. She grinned widely.

"Your attitude will be reported to Krajan, and he won't be so pleasant, huh? So, maybe you'd like to tell us right now *how* you got our Swat Team disabled? Nuked their implants with something, didn't you?"

He shook her head and tightened his grip. She stuck out her tongue. He glowered. "Think you're cute, huh? Cooperation and repentance might get you some lenience. And how about your clever little program for Spero's Bee, the one that let him evade us?" Anna continued grinning at the ceiling.

Rollins flung her head away, letting it go with a quick, painful twist. "No, you know what? Even though it would be a *real* pleasure to beat it out of you, I'm just going to let the probe do its work." He sneered. "Maybe we can have our little fun later."

He squinted at the captives and spoke to his squad. "All right, men. Take these traitors out of here and load them on the bus. They're all going to Police Interrogation."

The prisoners were prodded out the door shuffling slowly in their leg irons. One began to sing hoarsely. "How great is *our* God. Sing with me. How great…" He received a sound whack with a baton, but all began to join in: "How great, how *great*, is our God."

COMING HOME

Justin pounded the armrests on his Captain's chair. *What have I done? Yesterday I was an esteemed Director and today I'm a rebel on the run. Anyway, that's the way it looks, doesn't it? And a week will have gone by when I get back home from nineteen eighty six.*

He put his head in his hands. *A killer swat team? Didn't think it would be that bad. No telling what happened to my people after I rescued Professor Main.* Uncaring, the Bee droned on, sliding silently toward the twenty third century and his destiny.

And it's my QDT the soldiers invaded. Can't really predict the result—just too many unknowns. Justin tried to stretch out in his seat, but comfort was elusive. *Oh great, now I'm getting heartburn too.*

He belched, slouched back in the chair and sighed. *Well, what was I to do? Didn't really have any choice, did I? I had to save the Professor but for all I know, the police soldiers could be shooting everyone in sight right now. And here I am alone, just stewing in this Bee Capsule with no way to help them.* He gave the chair arm a sideways hit.

Justin squirmed around and reviewed possible scenarios. He had to admit that Spero and the new computer had done an amazing job of totally outsmarting him. *Sure I suspected the stolen Bee might be returned with an innocent person from the past, but Spero selected someone whom he knew in advance would live on. Crafty. Totally brilliant too was his idea of sending Professor Joseph Main himself, the founding father of Bee technology.* He closed his eyes and remembered the picture hanging in his office, thc older version of Professor Joseph Main with his happy grin.

Abruptly he sat up, pulled the keypad in his arm rest toward him and checked the arrival time: "Two days, eighteen hours of onboard time left to go," he said out loud. *Hard to believe Spero never told the young Joe about what he'd later become. In all fairness, I'm sure he couldn't have guessed there'd be an assassination squad on arrival. I wouldn't have. All Spero really knew for sure was that Joe was going to survive and return to nineteen eighty six. Can't change history. Clever.*

Justin stared at the fuzzy view-screen as the Moon made lazy circles around the Earth. He shrugged. *Anna turned out to be our surprise secret weapon after all. Bet even she didn't realize she had the power to block weapon ID chips, and drop an entire police squad like that. But wow, when she had to, she just did it.*

And none of us would have had a chance to save ourselves, much less Joe, if it weren't for Sarah. She took one huge personal risk by warning us. I hate to think what the police would do to poor Sarah if they found out. Justin slapped a hand over his eyes and bowed his head. *Oh dear God, please protect dear, precious Sarah. My whole team would've died trying to save the professor if it weren't for Sarah and Anna. Those two women literally saved our lives!*

Justin took a deep breath, slumped back in his seat and closed his eyes. *Sarah, yes.* A great grin slowly grew across his face. Sarah. He recalled her sweet comforting presence, the innocence of her beautiful green eyes, and—oh yes: that little squeeze of her hand. Her memories fluttered through his mind as though he were inhaling fragrant spring zephyrs.

A distressing thought interrupted the reverie. Anna had called him a *Creative*. Of course he wasn't from the lowly Humwa Class, but she called him a Creative, and the term was supposed to mean the same thing. *I've worked with these people and treated them as equals for years. Never thought much about how suppressed the Humwa really were until Anna showed me.*

An orange light bar appeared on the dash with a chime indicating sleep stasis was ready. He switched it off. *Aten, our "supreme" leader has been horrible to them in recent years. Now he even wants everyone to treat him like their god and savior. But Spero escaped, and now Joseph too. That's hugely embarrassing for Aten's administration.*

Justin turned in his seat and took out the soft green sleeping suit. *Well, at least I know this. In my heart I'm committed to everyone's equality and freedom, but now I might have to choose between supporting the Police State or joining the Humwa.* He hit his armrest again. *God, if I join them, I'll be the revolution.*

He leaned forward on his knees and replaced his face into his hands. The onboard computer responded to his distressed vital signs and initiated a programmed response. "All onboard systems are normal, Captain. Would you like to play a game of chess?"

Justin sighed. "No thanks." *You know what? I'm probably worrying way too much. By now every city in the world has seen the live video we sent out and they've all witnessed the swat team's attempted murder. The complicity of Margo and the Police Director is obvious. Bet they'll both be in jail when I get back with some new, apologetic Chairman sitting in Margo's place. Heck, maybe I'll be welcomed as a hero for exposing them.*

The onboard computer changed the wrap-around screen picture to a scene of rolling hills and flowing streams. Mood music began. It announced: "Captain, at this time I recommend that you prepare for stasis."

"Not yet. Terminate the music." There was the Moon swinging around the Earth on his view screen. *What if I'm wrong though? What possibilities did I miss? The Police Director will certainly get fired. Has to, right? But Chairman Margo's a political survivor. Bet she had a contingency plan to distance herself from the Swat Team.*

Justin grabbed his head with both hands, and shut his eyes tightly. "Aaaahh!" *There could even be a full blown revolution going on right now. Oh God, they'll probably expect me to lead it, too. Really wish I could talk to Sam right now.*

Justin jerked out the arm and leg exercisers from a side compartment. Working out calmed him down a little, but the inside of the Bee seemed to be getting smaller and quieter every moment. He stretched his arms out and discovered he could touch both its walls at the same time.

"Captain, you need to change clothes at this time."

"Shut up!" He threw his arm exerciser at the monitor. Justin stared in disbelief at the crack he'd made on its screen, and swatted his forehead. *Now I'm angry with a computer? You're losing it, Justin. Forget it. You'll find out what's going on when you get there. Live with it.*

He retrieved the exerciser and went back to his workout. *But there are some things I can control. I'm still the Director of the QDT after all. Be commanding. Stay in charge, Justin. Yeah!*

Exhaustion overcame him and he finally allowed himself a few hours of normal sleep. When he jerked awake it was June 6th 2066. Time-fixing down on Earth's surface was unsafe and banned for that time period, but he requested a pause in travel and put the Bee in orbit.

Justin made the hatch transparent and searched the Earth below. Bomb flashes and advancing radiation clouds marched relentlessly across his planet like a spreading plague of hatred. On the night side, orange glow balls would swell and subside at random. From this height they looked like fire flies on a warm Carolina evening. He shook his head. *Just had to see for yourself, didn't you Justin? Horrible. There's what happens when humans think they can make their own utopian destiny.*

"Attention, Captain. Our presence has been detected. A satellite killer missile has been launched against us from North America."

"How long do we have?"

"Thirteen minutes, Captain."

"I'll wait another five." Justin shook his head. *On the way back, Joe told me the United States was the envy of all nations: a free people in charge of their own destiny, but despised by the worlds dictators. It was "One Nation Under God." That's not what are schools are teaching. We're taught it was the spawn of the Devil and destroying it was the "will of God." Whose God?*

"Second missile detected, Captain. This one is from the Middle East, impact: fourteen point four minutes."

Justin meditated on the fireballs flaring and subsiding below. He was surprised to find himself quietly crying.

Abruptly he sat up straight. *Well, that was then, and it can't be changed. Now is the future--my future.* "Computer: full stasis procedure please. Resume travel plan."

Justin made one protocol change. He would wait for the receiving station to call him first. There might be an advance clue about to what to expect on the ground. He sighed and relaxed into his seat. For now, he would sleep--and hope for dreams of Sarah.

# # #

Onboard systems nudged Justin into awareness as the Bee approached a geosynchronous orbit. He promptly changed back into his work suit. The Bee's robotic arms had cleaned and pressed it and his beige, form fitting jacket looked like new.

There would be an inevitable hail from below when his presence was detected, but since he had to wait, he took out the telescope and peered down on Carolina Dome. *No smoke billowing up at least. Ah, there it is.* He focused on the line of structures down the hill from the Dome. *I wonder what'll happen to Saunders village when they discover it.*

It's incredible they've remained undetected for all these years.

"Acknowledging your orbital location. Please respond." *There's the automated voice from our QDT base. At least they didn't launch a missile at me.* His onboard computer responded: "Bee 76, Geosync 3, requesting retrieval, Dome 22."

"Bee 76: State your passenger manifest."

"Dome 22: One person, Director Justin 126. Sending 'ident' codes."

"Authorized. Proceed to primary arrival station."

"Acknowledged. Out"

Couldn't tell much from that, but everything's working normally. No people talking. Maybe my guys don't want to congratulate me on the open airways.

The Bee swooped down through patchy clouds on auto pilot, and without hesitation it emerged inside the QDT arrival chamber. Dead quiet for a moment. "Bang!" The Bee's particles snapped away. Justin flinched.

He searched in vain, trying to spot anyone through the one chamber window. The air began to hiss back into the room. *If there's any hard feelings here, the best plan is to be calm, assert my rank and sound self assured. Of course, I'll also be my charming, diplomatic self.*

He quickly shaved, and combed his wavy, yellow hair while the pressure outside equilibrated. With as much grace and dignity as he could bring to bear, Justin climbed out of the small hatch. He brought himself fully upright, straightened his jacket and looked admonishingly at the single police soldier who strode toward him. He raised a finger and spoke in a firm, scolding tone. "Officer, in this room you are required to wear a sterile clean suit over your uniform."

The soldier returned a smirk, and deftly fired his neural stunner into Justin's chest.

1988

Two years earlier, Joe and Melissa were blessed with an epiphany of love and mutual understanding. They discovered their hearts had long been, and would remain, inseparable, so it came as no surprise to their friends when they married six months after their first real date. While their monetary fortunes grew rapidly thanks to Spero's gift, both were conservative spenders. However, on Spero's advice, they did buy a large tract of Colorado wilderness. When Melissa was expecting, the newlyweds moved into a non-working farmhouse on the edge of their Ohio college town.

Canis clearly needed a second dachshund friend to manage the vermin in his now huge back yard and was blessed with a female dachshund named Calliente. It had taken some time for Joe's cat, Inertia, to reach a living arrangement with the dogs. The final working agreement was that Inertia was boss and he preferred to be left alone.

The cat was actually bigger than either of the dogs and, as they soon discovered, he had claws and was easily irritated.

Joe came up from his new basement wine cellar carrying a bottle of Washington State Merlot under one arm, Korbel Champagne under the other, and sporting a big grin.

He lifted the bottles over his head. “To success, Darling.”

Bolstered by his new work in particle physics, Joe had just been appointed a full Professor, and last year Melissa had been promoted to Associate Professor. But most important to her, was receiving a grant to search ancient artifacts along the western coast of the Americas. Spero’s information would finally be checked out. This was a controversial field, of course, and she had to endure playful chiding about her “surfer’s grant”.

The cork popped across the room, and Cally chased it, toenails clicking all the way down the hall. They laughed and clinked their glasses. “Melissa, I’m so looking forward to my paid sabbatical at Cal Tech. That way, Darling, I can also work as your part time Malibu assistant.”

Melissa produced a mock pout. “My work could take us down as far as Peru Sweetie, but you are welcome to come if you’re really serious about helping. And speaking of helping, why don't you finally go through those unpacked boxes from your old apartment? I'll bet there's a lot in there you can throw out."

"Oh, right. That'll be a fun way to spend the evening. Honey, I'll unpack that stuff when I set up my new office on Sunday, okay?"

Melissa took a gulp of champagne and cocked her head to one side. Her eyes glinted. "News flash, my Dear: The Humane Society Thrift Shop will be *so* happy when they see the size of our donation pile this weekend. And did you notice the dumpster I ordered?"

"Oh I know. You don't like my lawn chairs."

"They were your mothers from the 60's. They're frayed, hugely ugly, and a health hazard, and that's just the beginning, Mister."

"Shoot. Now I'll bet you want to donate my kitchen table too, right?"

Melissa snort-laughed. "Nah, wouldn't embarrass us by taking it there. It's from the fifties, has a hideous green Formica top, and one leg badly repaired with *duck tape*. Dumpster bound."

Joe slumped back in his chair meekly. "I sort of knew that one was history." He sighed. "I guess we really could afford to replace some furniture."

Melissa chuckled affably. "Duh--but listen, this is what's really on my mind. I woke up in the middle of the night thinking about some things you said a long time ago."

"My Millennium Falcon model stays. It's autographed by Hans Solo, and that's final."

Melissa laughed, and kicked out at his foot. "No, no. I know I'd never get *that* away from you, but just keep it in your den, OK? No, this is about that lady friend of yours in the computer, the one who had a crush on you."

"Connie? She did not. Well, I don't think really. Anyway she showed me how much I really loved *you,* remember?"

"Aaww, I know. That was so nice. But I never asked you about this." Melissa put her glass on the coffee table and leaned forward on the edge of the couch, leveling a squinty stare at her husband. "Was Connie actually able to put those arms she had outside the Bee and move things around?"

"Sure, she could reach out of the hatch with two of the arms about three feet. That's how she helped me get Spero inside when he was unconscious."

Melissa sat back and tousled her brown curls with one hand. Joe knew this to be a sign of dangerous ideas inside. She raised her index finger with a little wiggle. "Ah, yes. That's how she left her book and that CD disc too, of course. Let me guess. You found them in the bookshelf you used to have in the living room near the hallway, right?"

"Good guess. But okay, so what?"

"All right, here's what woke me up. My earlier memory of that shelf was that it was a complete mess just like the rest of your things, bless your heart. However, when we were packing up to move you out, that shelf was the most orderly thing in your apartment. Now, knowing you, I'm sure you weren't suddenly overcome with a neatness bug. It looked *womanly* neat."

"Yeah well, you're right. Connie probably just straightened it to attract my attention. You know, so I'd notice what she left me. The discs were right there on the top shelf next to the copied over Beatle's tape."

Now Melissa finished her glass and stared through the wall in thought. She put it down slowly, and leaned forward on her elbows. "Well then, you never really examined the *rest* of the things you had on your bookshelves, did you?"

"Of course not, but I'm sure I got everything she meant for me to see. Followed all Spero's clues, too. Why would she hide something else in another place?"

More hair tousling. "Now I have a mental image from when we were packing up your apartment. I can remember your bare hairy arm just sweeping off those shelves into one big box. As I recall, I got you to label it: 'LV-B case'."

"Wow, what memory you've got. Look, Mele, I'll put every bit of it away when I unpack, and neatly. I promise."

Melissa smiled. "Don't misunderstand. This isn't a complaint, Sweetie." She tilted her head and batted her eyelashes, "But, after dinner I'd like you to humor me a little. If you can find that particular packing box and haul it up from the basement, I'll do the dishes tonight."

Joe picked up her hand, kissed it, and poured more champagne. "Well, since you put it that way, of course Darlin. But first: here's a toast to you, your new grant, and to the 'Peruvian Riviera'."

Melissa clinked his glass. "Whatever you say, *Professor*."

2247

Justin's consciousness returned slowly, painfully. His temples throbbed like boils and his brain felt like steel wool. Gingerly he swung his feet off the cot and tried to focus on his surroundings, but his head kept wobbling. He lunged toward a nearby toilet and threw up. After a few gasping moments he felt better.

He rinsed his mouth out in the sink and rubbed his tender chest. *Oh yes, shot.* The room started spinning. Justin sat down again and leaned back on the head of the cot. He closed his lids, took a few measured deep breaths, and squinted for a look around. *Police jail cell, isolation type. No windows, just a slot way up there on the wall behind me.*

Past the bars, a blank, yellow corridor wall added to his confinement. *Dead silent out there, so probably no other cell is occupied.*

Justin flinched when a unexpected voice came from his brain implant: "I'm really sorry about the headache, Justin."

He grabbed his face with both hands. "Oh, shoot. That can't be," he cried out. The implant voice was only supposed to respond to thought questions from the owner. Save for emergency warnings, it had no ability to start a conversation.

"Justin, I know it doesn't sound like my voice but this is Anna. When they arrested you yesterday I knew the first thing would be a memory scan. Thank goodness I was close enough to you to erase some portions of it concerning myself, Sarah, and your knowledge of Saunders. I gave your memories back to you while you slept, but I'm new at using this ability. If your head hurts, it's mostly my fault. Sorry."

Justin staggered over to the bars and looked up and down the hall: dead end on his right, door to the left. "Well, my head's better after I threw up. Looks like I'm all alone in here."

"Don't speak out loud. Just think your words like you would ask your implant for information. I can't believe they stunned you, poor dear. They're recording every sound, so please practice talking through your implant."

Justin staggered to the sink, poured himself some water in a plastic cup but his wooziness returned so he sat down. He "spoke" through his implant. "*You continue to amaze me, Anna. Yet another new ability, huh? I suppose you're sitting at your QDT station?"*

"Don't I wish? No, I'm in a cell just like yours, but one level up. So is Sam, and all your department heads too--even your secretary. And it's all *your* fault, I might add."

"*Oh, thanks. My fault? How do you figure that*?"

"Because I could've easily put every storm trouper to sleep if you'd have let me, and taken their weapons too."

"*Anna, I spent two days going over scenarios. My best guess was that once all the world saw the vids of their attempted murder and the building take over, they'd back right down. Vids went out world wide, right?"*

"They did. But just half an hour later they had a doctored video version running with the claim that our live transmission was rebel propaganda—fake news."

"Anna, our live video feed coincided with the known time of the Bee's arrival. It had a verifiable security stamp for the media showing that it was absolutely not a recorded rebroadcast. Every news agency recognizes this authentication."

"Sure, but are you surprised that all Domes except three sent out the retraction and ran their fake story? The

Supreme Directorate must have even more control that we thought. Fact is, they're calling all the shots."

"Maybe so, but three domes did keep the truth going out, right?"

"Yes: South Africa, Argentina, and Cal Domes. They kept running the undoctored story, included expert commentary, and even sent their part out to the rest of the world. That only lasted two minutes before network central pulled the sat feed on all three of them. No transmissions of any kind from those cities since. 'Technical difficulties' sounds too feeble for even the most gullible, don't you think?"

"So now I suppose everyone in the world is blaming me for our building being stormed and letting a criminal escape."

"I can't laugh through this communication link, but know that I just did. You're so modest, Justin. Your way of handling things actually saved all our lives at QDT. There wasn't even an injury. Had I been in charge, my actions would've tipped them off about my abilities prematurely, and given them an excuse for a full military response."

Justin began to pace his cell. "*Saving lives was my priority, but it is my fault we're all in jail and at their mercy.*"

"Nonsense. You're our hero here at QDT, the whole world, really. We'll all follow your orders. You said to just 'surrender'. It wasn't what we wanted to do, but we did, and it was absolutely the right decision-- a beautiful one. I see that now. We all do."

"*Well yeah, but now we're all rotting in jail.*"

"OK, but how're you doing? My cell has pastel walls, sweet music, a soft bed, and a window with a lovely view."

"*Lucky you. But I suppose SD will keep us here indefinitely. They'll probably replace us all, or worse. We're alive for now, but it's a pretty powerless situation, isn't it?*"

"Don't be so glum, Justin. They don't know I can monitor all their conversations while I lie back and sip lemonade."

"*Oh, so they're buttering you up, but can you tell me what they did to our video?*"

"Sure, boss. Only kidding about my room and the lemonade, by the way. These cells are almost as bleak as my assigned Humwa living quarters. Ever visited one?"

"*Can't say I have. That bad, huh?*" Justin slid his feet off the cot and tried some stretch exercises. "*But you want plush? You should see the villas behind the walled compound where Margo and the Chief live. Anyway, tell me about their cover-up.*"

"Well, the altered vid was pretty good for a rush job. First, they changed the professor's face to some fearful character with a black beard. When Professor Main was actually raising his hands to surrender they made it look like he fired a weapon with one hand and held some sparkling rod in the next. Viewers are supposed to believe this rod was the secret weapon that dropped the police. They didn't have to retouch the scenes of the building being stormed since their actions then appeared to be justified."

Justin found he could stand up on his shaky knees and went to the bars. "*So most everyone believed that crap?*"

"Well, yeah many did at first. Remember, a lot of people actually think Aten is 'our god and savior', so they don't doubt the SD, but I think most are beginning to wise up. There are flaws in the fake vid that will eventually show it for what it is. Truth is their actions are actually *producing* a revolution of sorts when there wasn't one in the first place, especially in South Africa. I can hear our Police Chief, and he's really upset about it."

Justin stood on his cot and tried to peer through the slot in the outside wall. "*Knowing Margo, a little poison gas might be her ultimate solution.*"

"Now Justin, stop being so pessimistic. The administration is actually quite afraid of you and this unknown weapon threat of yours. But that's just me, isn't it? Tee, he. *I'm* you're scary weapon. They mind-probed everyone at the QDT and found no clue about how their soldiers were dropped, and that really frightened them."

"Ha, ha. So, no one knew it was you, not even Sam."

"Right, and get this: there's about a hundred protestors in front of this police building right now and not a one of them is Humwa. The admin is *really* scared of protests, don'cha know."

"*You're not kidding? That many on our side?*"

"Absolutely, and I like it you said 'our side'. You know what? You've got lots more fans, Mr. 'curly locks'. It's a real old fashioned spontaneous thing. They're chanting: 'Try 'em or release 'em.' and 'Who's to blame? Who's to blame?' They keep repeating it over and over. It's kind of musical. Compelling, too." "*Anna, you're such a gem. I'm feeling much better already. Is Sarah's OK? Have they charged us with anything?"*

"Sarah's fine, and you'll be glad to know they never suspected her involvement either. Officially the rest of us are being held on charges of aiding and abetting a known criminal. That's laughable, isn't it? The God meetings like the one she attends are convinced Spero's escape was God's will. They believe he's been selected for some special mission."

"*And me?"*

"Sorry, but prophets seem to be silent on your fate, Boss. However, I do know that Margo and the police are about to meet in the 'war room' upst…"

"What? What is it, Anna?"

"Sorry, Justin. Gotta sign off. Someone's coming."

ARCHEOLOGIST DIG

Melissa sat cross-legged on the living room floor, dug through the cardboard box, and laid out its contents on the floor with meticulous care. Aided by Joe's sketchy memory of his bachelor bookshelf, she arranged everything in rows on the floor corresponding to their likely former shelf location. "There, now I think we're ready."

Joe sighed. "Well, dear, I think I've had a breakthrough already."

Melissa's head snapped up, intense hazel eyes trained on him. "Really? What?"

"Until this moment I never realized how truly, truly compulsive archeologists are."

"Now pay attention, Sweetie. If you're going to help in California you need to know how important patience and organization are when you're searching for long lost things. So far I don't see anything unusual, but we should play each of these tapes, at least from their beginning. Perhaps something's been added to another one of them."

"Mele, that's silly. What makes you think Connie would leave anything else for me, especially something hidden? You saw the note she left me, and her mushy romance novel CD."

"We'll just see, won't we?" Melissa began inspecting audiocassettes with one hand while she scratched her dog's brown chest with the other. Calliente lay on her back air walking through the process.

Melissa angled her gaze toward Joe and tossed her short hair toward one side. "And Connie's novel wasn't mush. It was so much more than just a love story, Joe. Didn't you see how she explored the actual foundation that loving couples use to build a relationship? She talked about the husband-wife-God triangle of mutual support. For me it was certainly a new twist on the 'love triangle'. It even made me think about how a mutual belief in God holds a marriage together."

"But that's never been your thing, has it?"

"God? No, but she did show how the responses of ones mate can reverberate in that kind of a three way relationship. Very insightful I thought, didn't you?"

“Nope.” Joe sidled over behind her and went down on his knees. “Cause I already know all about getting a reverberating response.” He gave a quick nip to her neck.

With a screech and a swat, Melissa laughed and batted him away. “Listen, after all you’ve told me about Connie, and reading her book, I have no trouble believing she was an actual woman, or at least she certainly had the mind of one, right?”

“Oh, yes.”

“Well, if it had been me, I would have also left something personal for you. That’s my intuition. After all, you three went through a lot together.”

Joe sat down with another sigh and sat back against the couch. “Maybe you’re just jealous. Well all right, I guess I could help out. Would it make you happy if I threw out some of my old stuff in there?”

Melissa had started to listen to the cassettes with ear phones, but gave him a thumbs-up smile.

Joe examined the rows of his possessions and began to toss “dead” pens and convention souvenirs into an empty box against the wall. He banked in a Koala Bear paperweight. “Two points! And here’s a two-year-old student workbook to a course I don’t even teach anymore.”

He chuckled. “Look Honey, it’s labeled ‘tomorrow’s lesson plan’, but I never even used it.”

Joe tried to scale the large soft cover folder into the box, but it flew open scattering papers and photos on the floor.

Melissa screeched, paralyzing Joe.. “Ahh-HA!” She lunged for them, earphones flying away, and came up with two pictures and a piece of white paper with handwriting. She jumped up, plunged the paper into her shirt and eluded her pursuing husband. “See, here’s a picture of you and Spero in space suits standing on a orangey-red seashore—got to be on ancient Mars, huh? The other one…” she convulsed in laughter. “The other one is you and Spero playing Neanderthals with spears.”

Melissa scaled the photos at Joe. “Hey, look, she drew a smile face in the margin. I love Connie.”

Joe glanced at the pictures. “Oh quit laughing.” He renewed his pursuit.

Melissa took out the paper. “It’s a note from Connie, all right and it’s on *your* stationary.” She hopped and twisted around the room, deftly evading him as she read:

Hi Joe. I am assuming you will be opening these books for your classes next week. Just wanted to thank you from the bottom of my heart for accepting me as a real person. It meant so much to me. I'm not sure Spero ever did, and I probably would've gone crazy without you and your genuine concern. My intuition tells me that you and Melissa will soon be a happy, loving couple.

Melissa put one hand on her heart, and held the paper straight down with the other. "Aaaaa" She pointed her finger at Joe with a "there, see" look before going on.

Its too bad Spero won't be able to keep these photos of our adventures, but I hope you and Melissa enjoy them. My only regret is not being able to visit with you two. By now you must understand I'm a hopeless romantic. Well, duhh. I write love stories.

Joe continued the futile pursuit of his wife around the room trying to glimpse the back page of the note, but with spins and twists she kept it out of his reach.

Anyway Joe, I wanted to give you something to say thank you just from me. I came up with two things. First, the samples you collected from Mars are labeled "A(Mars)" and "B(Mars)". I think you know "A" is water and air, and "B" has that little creature you captured. Now, "C(air)", and "D(water)" are not the duplicates you might suppose. They are samples Spero took on Earth at the same 235 million BC time frame. Comparing them should be really interesting, don'cha think?

The other present is really from Gorilla, our grumpy super-comp, and me. It's the equation our scientists use to express the unified field. I've included some explanatory notes but notice that there's no character for 'time'. Remember it doesn't exist. Well, speaking for me, time really does exist cause I miss you guys all the time.

Here's wishing you and Melissa the wonderful and joy filled life you deserve.

Love, Connie

Melissa finally thrust the paper into Joe's chest. He fell backward onto the couch staring open mouthed at the equation. He studied it, mumbling letters and numbers with sing-song emphasis. Finally Joe looked up, his voice a hoarse whisper. "OK, you were right, darling. Now I have an awesome respect for women's intuition."

MARGO 023

Chairman Margo had assembled a meeting of Key Personnel in the highly secure Police Conference room. Gathered around the conference table were the Director of her personal Security Force plus its Head of Operations, Police Chief Ahab, Retrieval Chief Cecil, and the head of the Police Science Lab. They were arguing with Director of Health, Susan, when Chairman Margo entered in a rush flanked by personal bodyguards. She motioned for everyone to sit down, and began to speak before she reached her seat at the head of the table.

"People, first of all you should know that this is not a 'war room' conference, but it's quite clear to me that the Humwa are deliberately provoking this legitimate government. I'm going to start by first telling you what I know, and then what I need to find out. Hopefully we'll finalize a plan today and put down these rebellious seeds before things get worse."

Still standing, she slid her chair aside. Her eyebrows slowly lowered. “It is important for you to know that there is now unrest at every city Dome on the planet, so don’t think for a *minute* that we are acting alone. Supreme Director Aten has personally ordered Police Chief Ahab to coordinate resources with me. Needless to say, he’s expecting swift results.”

Murmurs circulated around the conference table. Margo tolerated these for a few moments, before she leaned forward and slapped her hand down on the surface. The effort released a clump of gray-black hair which dangled down on one side. Her voice tone changed into a stressed, school bus driver addressing unruly children: “Look people. I realize you have questions, but if everyone gets to work immediately, we’ll soon have answers.”

Margo glowered into every ones eyes as though they were hiding secrets behind their faces. “I do hope you understand that this was a Humwa plot, a plot that engineered the theft of our Bee *and* its return, *and* the escape of a conspirator. Not only that, but the plan was intended to make our Police look unlawful and abusive before the eyes of the world. None of this happened by chance. That much I know." She turned toward the Chief. "Ahab, tell them about Abel 119."

The Chief slumped back casually and raised his great, furrowed head. "We mind-probed all of Spero's recent contacts. Dede 980 gave us a list. They were all negative except for Abel 119. He had witnessed Spero's written plan for revolution." "Ooohs" went around the table. "He read the plan once to his wife and burned it."

"And the plan is?"

"His memory was vague, and some things were ridiculous. For instance, Spero wanted a sports field in the flat area near the airport, and he wanted to have concerts and plays in our assembly hall; God meetings too. Can you believe that? In *Sunrise Hall*, for Aten's sake."

"Just drivel, Chief. Those are useless Humwa dreams. We've all heard that garbage before."

"True, but blasphemous. Worse, he actually had a plan to rally the world around a voting democracy and remove Aten. *That* my dear, is the really radical stuff. Abel liked his ideas too—mind-probe showed it. Our military tribunal beheaded him yesterday."

Susan squeaked and covered her mouth. "His--his wife. Is she under arrest too?"

"Her memory scan was so full of terror we couldn't get a reliable reading, but she is probably innocent."

Susan's shoulders slumped. "Well, thanks for that anyway."

"Yes, the woman was hysterical. Tribunal gave her Aten's mercy."

"Oh good. Where is she? I'll see if I can help her."

Ahab turned to Susan, his lip curled. "Her death by injection was quick and painless. Revolutionary bodies are all sent to Aten at the SD for his victory ceremony."

Susan slid back in her seat with an open mouth. Margo leaned forward, hands on the table. Her steely gaze moved from one person to the next. "So, back to finding solutions. The next thing we need to find out is this: what new weapon do they have? What is this device that defeated our best Police Units? Hugo?"

A slight, balding man cleared his throat. He began twitching as he looked around at the stern faces focusing on him. "Hugo 244, Police Science. Well, ahem. We have examined all eight of the weapons involved and determined that their comp-chips were altered. Of course the knives don't have chips." He looked for smiles, saw none.

"Well, ahem. As you know each weapon can only be fired by the officer who owns it since the signature ID of his brain implant has to match the weapon chip. All the weapons were altered to empower a different authorized user, a person not on our police force."

"So, that traitor is not in the room, I assume." Margo nodded her head. "I understand that the weapons were still on the floor when our reinforcements arrived. Perhaps you have a Creative plotter hiding in your Police Department after all." She studied Ahab's expressionless face for a moment.

"Hugo, were you able to determine which of the conspirators could have actually fired those weapons? Name this man: the one who could have picked these guns up from the floor and turned them back on us. I hope he's still alive so we can all enjoy a trial and a slow public death in Park Central."

"Yes, Ma'am, I know whose implant ident it was, but it wasn't someone who'd seize the guns. Trust me, the name's really not important."

"Well Hugo, now you trust *me*. We all want to know anyway." Margo eyes narrowed. "Was it someone we would recognize, like Justin for instance, or was it just some random person we wouldn't know?"

"No, you know the person."

"Oh, for Aten's sake, who is it?"

"It's you, Ma'am--you. All the weapons were set so that only you could fire them."

Margo looked like she had something stuck in her throat. She slowly slid down into her chair, her eyes blazing off into space.

Hugo broke the stunned silence. "This switch probably did not occur at the Police Station. All officers checked their weapons in test firing mode when they dressed for duty and had them on their person at all times since then."

Margo swore under her breath and composed herself. A pained smile replaced the anger. "Well then Hugo, can you tell us how the Humwa pigs accomplished this taunting little switch?"

"No Ma'am."

Margo spoke through her teeth and nodded her head. "We would all like it if you made a *guess,* Hugo."

"Yes Ma'am. They probably used a high-energy wireless beam for reprogramming. Of course they would need the access codes on the weapon chips. But given that, if they were physically close enough, it would be possible in theory to reprogram each weapon. We notified our manufacturer, and they are working on an upgrade to make wireless chip access more difficult."

"I'm sure you're right, Hugo. You usually are. Any evidence of where this machine was set up at the QDT?"

"No ma'am, but transceivers like the one I suspect could be moved in and out of an area quickly."

"I see. And the same device was used to make our men unconscious, I suppose?"

"No Ma'am, nothing like that would work on shielded implants."

After a moment of silence Margo resumed her condescending tone. "We are all waiting for your next guess, Hugo."

"I--I really don't know. If I was forced to guess I'd say it would be some kind of a focused magnetic pulse weapon. That might discharge our implants but the police ones are shielded for magnetism and audio bursts. A strong magnetic pulse could cause temporary unconsciousness, but they would have to have a really large and obvious device.

Besides, it would have affected everyone else in the room including the person you were trying to kill."

"Apprehend, Hugo. Not kill," Margo added through clenched teeth. "And he was a primitive. No implant."

Hugo sat down nodding and gesturing. "Of course, of course, you're right M'am. It wouldn't have affected him".

"Well, keep working on it. We need to find out more about these nasty weapons of theirs."

The retrieval Chief rose to his feet. "But this 'primitive', as it turned out, was actually the genius who made QDT possible in the first place, wasn't he? I'm assuming my Department was never included in your plans since this was intended to be a political murder and not really a retrieval, correct?"

"Cecil 240! Sit down. You're only here to help answer questions if we need you, not start some new attack of your own."

Cecil continued anyway. "We all realize that we have positions appointed by you, Madame Chairman, and all of us share your desire to preserve our government. Detection and Retrieval has been finding and returning escaped Humwa for generations. Hundreds of these people have been interviewed, scanned, even tortured in my

Department, but we have yet to see any evidence of a planned rebellion, that frivolous paper not withstanding. And this man who arrived, admittedly a creative type person from his own time, was unarmed and passive as we all know."

Margo pointed to his chair. "Sit down Cecil. This is not a post mortem of our strategy. We didn't need your detection or retrieval because this man was being delivered to us. There was every advance reason to believe that he would probably be hostile, and the presence of unknown weapons bares that out."

Cecil sat slowly, shaking his head.

"And as to politics, it's not your field so don't waste our time with your rhetoric. Our immediate problem right now is the riot going on in the streets out there."

But Cecil was not about to back down. He looked up Margo with narrowed eyes. "Politics no, but I do know people, and I know our Creatives. Those are legitimate protesters out there, not rioters. And they're *our* people, not the Humwa."

Margo sounded strained but spoke softly. "That may be, but still, its all because of what the Humwa did. It's what they *did*..." Her voice trailed off as she sat down. Her lips began to tremble, and she waved for the Police Chief to speak.

Rather than stand, the hulking Chief eased to the edge of his chair and placed folded hands on the table. His gaze slowly moved around the table. Finally, he turned slightly and faced Margo. "We are in no danger whatever, Madame Chairman. My forces are deliberately ignoring these lightweight protesters. They'll grow tired and go home eventually."

Margo shook her head, her long hair curl flaying from side to side. "But what if you're wrong, Ahab? What if the protests get worse?"

The Chief smirked. "Cecil's right. These people would never consider joining any revolution with the Humwa even if one existed. They just need to be handled the right way. But if they did try something, we have a secret weapon of our own to deal with unruly crowds. Don't worry."

"You were to tell me *immediatel*y if you had a recommendation." Margo snapped. "Well, what are you suggesting is the *right* way? Punishment shackles for everyone?"

This seemed to amuse the Chief. Smiling for the first time, he replied: "No, my recommendation is simply to release every prisoner you have and put them back to work. We have no hard evidence against them, and we'll learn a lot more by careful surveillance. Aten will be pleased when there are no more protestors out there. You *do* want to please him don't you*?"*

The Directors had never seen their steely Chairman in such an emotional state. Margo felt her hands shaking and clasped them to hide it. She appeared ill and on the verge of tears. Susan 401, who was also her personal physician, got up and went over to her. She put her arm gently on Margo's shoulders and was not rebuffed. "We all understand the terrible stress you have gone through in these past few days, Margo, but it appears hopeful now. All of this seems to be dying down now, doesn't it?"

Fire snapped back into Margo's eyes and she brushed away Susan's arms. "You all know *nothing.* Only Ahab and I know the real truth, an awful truth…" The Chief swerved toward her glowering, his index finger raised. Margo gave him an assuring wave off. "It--it's just that it's all on our shoulders right now," she said. "We have to keep the peace here at all costs. Aten must be pleased--or else…"

FLIGHT PLAN

The high-wing Cessna seaplane droned on up California's North coast only a hundred feet above the foamy breakers below. It bounced and yawed as gusts from an onshore breeze toyed with the craft. Joe leaned over Melissa from the back seat and pointed to a rocky cliff face. "How about that one? I can see a cave for sure."

Melissa lifted her binoculars to study it. "It's an old sea cave all right, but it's too low. That was the problem with the second and fifth ones we explored. Remember the sea level has changed a lot in thirty thousand years and it was highest twenty thousand years ago. From now on we'll only look at caves above fifty feet unless, of course, you're really only here for your new sea shell collection."

"OK, boss," Joe said. He gave his wife a brief shoulder squeeze. "You still think Spero might be right about North American settlements, don't you?"

The plane lurched to one side with the turbulence. The pilot announced: "Sorry, guys, it's bouncy on slo-flight. We'll have to break off and refuel in ten minutes."

Melissa pointed to a spot ahead. "OK, Jack, but I like the looks of that high cliff wall we're coming to. Can you get us in a bit closer?" Jack gave them a "thumbs-up", throttled the engine back even further, and pulled the flap lever up a notch.

Melissa pressed her face against the window. "At first I was thinking that since there really were settlements in Monte Verde Chile fourteen thousand years ago, why not just look for something there. But, you're right. Those folks had to get ten thousand miles down the coast, and probably most wouldn't go all the way.

She put her hand on the glass. "Hey! Look at *that* cave. It's just ten feet from the top. Looks huge, and its got shrubs in front." Melissa passed the glasses to Joe. "Jack, I want to drop a marker on top. We can't risk climbing this one from the bottom with all our stuff."

The pilot replied, "Will you take responsibility, professor? I'll have to buzz the cliff, and I see a cabin nearby."

Melissa chuckled. "Jack, if anyone complains I'll tell them I had the controls." She reached under her seat and pulled out what looked like a large lawn dart. It sported a yellow flag on top, and the middle bulged with a black box.

Jack's broad grin announced he was relishing the chance to show off his Air Force expertise. The plane's engine roared, and they circled up and out to sea. Jack banked sharply and plummeted toward the top of the cliff. Half way down he cut the engine back and they floated down quietly as if they were going to land on top.

Melissa released her seat belt, opened the door, and fearlessly propped one foot out on the wing strut. As they swooped down, she threw the dart and Joe quickly grabbed her belt. "There. Bulls-eye! Oh Joe, I really like the way this cave looks."

Joe hauled her back into the seat. "Darling, please!"

Jack pushed full throttle again, banked away to gain altitude and swiveled his head to face them. "OK guys, where're we going to refuel? There's a field nearby in Trinidad, but after that I better take you back down the coast. Soon it'll be dar--oh look back there. Someone's waving at us from the cliff."

"Jack, you're off duty after we put down. We'll be staying in Arcata for the night and renting a car. I'm not going to lose two days. My grad students will drive up with the van, but I want to start on that site first thing in the morning."

After they landed, Jack gave them his aviation chart and marked the spot for them. He wished them luck with a grinning comic salute, and flew off leaving them to search for a rental car at the small airfield. Melissa had hoped for a Jeep, but had to settle for a sedan. She shrugged and whispered to Joe," Sure hope off-roading won't be necessary in that thing."

"You really like this cave site, don't you, Honey."

"It's hopeful, Joe. The cave's high enough to have been dry during the recent inter-glacial ocean, and it would have been climbable from below especially when the sea was higher. If I were a primitive fisherman, I'd be tempted to make a camp site there.

"Melissa, you do remember that I don't have a whole lot of time left."

"Yes, I know you have to get back to Ohio in a few days, but now is when I could really use your help, at least until my students get their bums out of the library and show up. Jack said there's a chance of rain tomorrow, so I'll be doing some shopping before supper. You can rest up at the motel."

"Hey, no problem. I'm hoping for a nice dinner out and some TV. But knowing you, what I'm really worried about is the time you'll want to get started tomorrow."

Melissa chortled. "We're up at five, soldier."

ALONE

Justin finished with his morning jumping jacks and pushups, sat down on the cool cell floor, and leaned against the wall to catch his breath. *It's been three mornings since Anna told me they were releasing prisoners. Not a word since. Apparently they meant everyone but* me, *and Anna must be out of communication range. Maybe their plan is just to let me rot here until I go insane. Shouldn't be long.*

Justin slid the stool, his only piece of movable furniture, against the wall. He had discovered that on tip toes he could see straight out the wall slot. Not much angle up or down, but at least there was some contact with the outside world. He noted that the sun came in early in the morning so his wall faced east. He knew this building. Only one side had a roof overhang and his slot was in the shade a few hours later. *That would put me directly over the main entrance.*

He turned his ear toward the glimmer of light. *Feels good to hear someone out on the street--actual human voices, but I can't make out any words. There used to be protesters chanting something, but it's pretty quiet now.*

He got down, kicked the stool over, and went over to hang on the cell bars and sulk. He stared at the closed door at the end of his hall. *It's like they're taunting me. Nobody ever comes here, nobody. Sure would like to see a person—Sarah would be my first choice. Wait, she probably thinks I'm traitor and a failure. Worse, maybe she doesn't even care.* He kicked at the bars and felt a shot of pain when his shin hit the lower crossbar.

A knee high panel began to slowly creak open midway down the corridor. An aluminum tray with a pile of dry pellets emerged. It was in the grasp of a small wheeled, faceless robot. It motored to the center of the hall. The bot swiveled ninety degrees and gradually moved toward his cell, swiveled again and lowered the tray to a slot under the bars. *Twice a day it comes out of that little panel with what they call food--disgusting food. I'd like to reach out and smash the dumb thing. Course then, I'd starve. Yup, I'll be a blubbering idiot in no time.*

He kicked the tray to one side, returned to his cot, sat, and rested his head in his hands. Big sigh. *I thought self-respecting political prisons beat people up and shouted at them. Actually I wish they'd give me some of that--maybe demand I confess to something. At least that would be interesting, but if they're gonna kill me anyway, I just wish they'd get it over with.* He slapped his cheeks. *Crazy talk. Just three days in solitary and your already thinking crazy, Justin. Time to start thinking sane again.*

He bent his knees up off the cot, and closed his eyes. *Okay, Margo and the rest of them think I'm a Humwa now. Why do these people make the Administration so angry?* He pulled the rubbery thing that was supposed to be a pillow over his head. *Well, let's see. Humwa do meet in private. Margo hates that. They play secret games, write, paint, create things, and enjoy music. What they don't do is pay any homage to Aten. Wait, that's it. What the Administration hates most is their secret God meetings. Worshiping God--that's the only offense they'll actually* kill *people for. Wonder why.*

Justin heard something—faint voices. *It's coming from the wall slot.* He hurried to get back up on his stool and turned his ear toward the sound. He could just make it out. A grin spread across his face. They were shouting "Free Justin. Free Justin."

The next afternoon, Justin's stomach told him there had been no meal delivered. He considered that starvation might be their new tactic, but suddenly he was startled by a clock-clocking sound. Someone was *walking* down his hallway. The light rapid paces suggested it was a woman. He jumped to the bars to face his visitor.

DÉTENTE

Margo stood before him wearing a wry smile. She moved her face close to his and squinted. "I suppose, pretty boy, I'm to assume you've no idea why your actions brought us this total disaster."

"I just followed protocol, Ma'am."

"Aten is not pleased. Your memory scan was certainly clean, but there were some suspiciously fuzzy areas. Some other Humwa at the QDT had the same pattern, so we know there's something fishy is going on."

She cocked her head to one side and studied his expression. "Obviously someone in your department had to have carefully planned for that Bee arrival, complete with hidden video camera, huh? OK Justin, why don't you tell me how it's possible that no one seems to know a thing?"

Justin stared at her, his face drained of emotion. Margo stamped her foot, dropped the bag she was carrying, and grasped the bars. "It is impossible for you not to have known, and *unbelievable* that everyone at QDT has innocent memory scans. You've found some way to alter those scans. I know you did."

Justin calmly looked down at her angry pout. He shrugged, and returned a "Mona Lisa" smile.

"Oh come on! I know when I'm being duped. Of course we faked the video of Professor Main holding a weapon. But still, he had to have one, or someone did. Some clever little gadget Spero made, perhaps? Devious fellow he was." Silence.

Margo took a step back and sighed. "OK, just answer one thing honestly for me. Are you, or are you not, part of any Humwa group planning to overthrow my Administration?"

"No." For another few moments they searched one another's blank expressions.

Margo shook her head and removed a large old-fashioned iron key from her pocket. "Strangely, I believe you." She unlocked his cell and looked up to answer his quizzical look. "Mem-chip locks can all be circumvented." She swung the door open. "These old locks are actually safer."

“We’re not done talking.” Margo flashed him an angry glance. “Follow me.” She handed him the bag she brought, and they exited into the next corridor. “You look terrible.” She pointed to a door. “Shower and shave. Change of clothes in the bag. When you’re done meet me behind the red door at the end of the hall.”

When Justin was ready, he knocked and entered. His ears told him the room was soundproofed. Margo sat waiting at a small table. “Are you releasing me, Margo?”

She motioned to a chair. “Yes, and you’ll go back to work tomorrow, but only if you promise to be on good behavior. Two things. Aten wants your whole Department to show up at morning worship before the gong rings, and put the four-place Bee development program on a top priority. Get on it. Water or Tea? Crackers, perhaps a sandwich?”

Justin guzzled the water. “All of them. Thank you. So, I am not being charged?”

Margo poured out two cups of tea. “We dropped the aiding and abetting charge. Officially you were just held for questioning. Unofficially, consider yourself disciplined for taking unauthorized actions.”

"It is authorized protocol as well as our written law to return someone to their own time immediately, Margo. It is not protocol to shoot them on arrival."

"Stun. They told me they would stun him for the mind probe."

"Four stuns would kill a horse. The one I got almost killed me." Justin aggressively chomped on the sandwich she pushed over to him.

"Yes, well those troops were a bit more enthusiastic than I expected, but I still don't think they meant to kill the man. We may never know. Anyway, I'm sorry we didn't get our mind probe of Professor Main."

Justin's mouth was full of food. "But you did get it, Margo. He volunteered to have it and I stored the data in Bee 76. You could've just asked me."

Genuinely surprised, the Chairman sat upright. "Really! That wasn't in *your* probe, and that proves yours was blocked, and now your memory is restored." She tilted her head and grinned. "Maybe we should scan you again?"

He grimaced, but she said, "Only kidding. Anyway, that's the first good news I've heard today. Thank you for that, Justin."

“Yeah, but it won’t do you much good. Spero kept the Professor from knowing his location. He thought it was in the Mediterranean area, but that would be conjecture. I thought the most interesting thing was the new computer program, but Joe said it erased itself before his arrival, right?”

Margo relaxed and put her cup down. She spread her hands out on the table, and gave Justin a look of genuine concern. “That computer is being examined in the police lab. I’m sorry if I misjudged you, Justin. Perhaps you were misguided and thought you were just helping friends. The behavior of the troops must have been frightening. I realize that you were only trying to do what you thought was the right thing. But tell me this honestly: was there any kind of a weapon on Professor Main?”

“Nope. I scanned him for our technology, and the scan of his apartment was negative too. Also you’ll see that the probe I did showed no weapon in his memory.”

“Good. Justin, my intuition tells me that you wouldn’t be part of revolutionary violence, so I believe you. But it also tells me you’re still concealing things from us. Do you know you talk in your sleep?”

Justin felt a sudden frisson of fear. *Oh God, did I give something away?*

Margo squinted her eyes. “But all you kept mumbling about was my *Secretary*.”

She shook her head at Justin’s smiling face. “I know you two have had something going, but listen, don’t either of you do anything to help the Humwa or you’ll regret it.”

Margo gestured to the door. “I guess you’ll be glad to be going home?”

Justin stood, grinning, but unbelieving.

“At the end of the next corridor the guards will show you to an official car. It will take you directly to your compound. No jogging through town just yet, and promise me you’ll assure your adoring crowd out there that all is well and they should go home too.” He smiled and nodded.

Sunshine blinded him as the doors opened. After days of dark, solitary confinement, the newly-released Director was hardly prepared for the sudden onslaught of lights, noise, and people, lots of people. A celebrating throng ran up the police steps and surrounded him. Some shook his hand, some hugged, and some patted him on the back. One woman kissed him on the lips. They were all chanting: “Justin, Justin, Justin.”

WAKE UP CALL

Joe lay surrounded by a peaceful, gray sleep-cocoon. Beyond the safety of his warm, dry wrappings, he was dimly aware of pleasant sounds: wind gusts and rain sheeting against the window. He felt a tapping on his foot, squirmed to a new place, and retracted his foot into the cocoon. Ahhh--it stopped. Warm and quiet.

Something grabbed his foot, and there was a voice. "Honey, I let you sleep as long as I could. They start breakfast here at five forty five. Up, up, *up*."

Bloodshot eyes oozed out from beneath the pillow. "Sweetie, cough--it's black, and pouring rain out there." His hoarse voice croaked, "Come on back in here, I'll keep you warm."

Melissa thumped down beside him, bouncing him up on the cheap mattress and pulled the pillow off his face. "No, no Dear. School day, today. We've got to check out our site before the van gets up here from San Francisco."

Joe rolled his eyes up at Melissa. She was dressed and bright-eyed. With a groan he hoisted himself up on his elbows. “Oh, why did I marry a morning person?” She smiled and scratched under his jaw line for a second, and deftly avoided a clumsy “gotcha” grab. “OK, OK, I’m getting up. But, we can’t dig mud in this *rain,* right? We have to wait for it to stop.”

Melissa skipped over to the wall and turned on a very bright overhead light. Joe’s face scrunched. “Oh, no, rain is *good*, dear. This way we can see how dry our old sea cave is. If it’s covered in a sea of mud, I promise you can go back to bed. But, look at this.” She held up a bright yellow slicker. “Jack was right about the forecast. I got us some pull over boots and ponchos when I went shopping last night.”

She shook the poncho. “See, you’ll be warm and dry.”

Slowly, Joe swung his legs out of bed. “Uggh. I hope our host wasn’t kidding when he said his Spanish omelets were worth dying for”.

Melissa put a knee on the edge of the bed and reached for Joe’s ears. “That’s my boy, finally waking up, I see.” Her mistake. With a loud growl, Joe grabbed her waist and twisted her into the bed. Tussling, shrieking, tickling, kissing, and slapping ensued before Melissa could slither out of his grasp. She tossed him his clothes. “Incorrigible! As if last night wasn’t enough for you.” She laughed. “Not a bit of respect for a genteel woman, and a pregnant one at that.”

By six-thirty their Taurus was heading north. Joe drove and Melissa directed their turns with the help of Jack’s map. Fortunately, the rain had quieted to a steady drizzle. After an hour they were making their way through winding side roads. She took out her beacon detector and announced she had a faint signal. “It’s really weak, Joe. Either the battery’s failing, or it got washed down the cliff last night.”

Their little car bounced along narrow, muddy roads as the locator signal directed them ever closer toward the ocean. The terrain was rough and almost uninhabited. “There! Over there.” Melissa motioned to a dirt drive. The ocean had appeared through the trees and beckoned them to a field beyond a parked trailer.

Joe turned and closed one eye. “This is private property, Mel. We’d be trespassing if we just walked in there.”

"Nonsense. I'll ask permission first. Of course if we don't get it, *then* we'll be trespassing." Joe chuckled and shook his head. They got out of the car, pulled up their poncho hoods, and headed for the humble dwelling. Melissa glanced at her locator, smiled at Joe, and poked her finger toward the rusted trailer.

A large white cat scurried underneath as they neared the door. Lucky for them the occupant turned out to be a college girl living in a cheap rental. She had picked up their beacon and had stashed it under her kitchen sink. Her boyfriend had been taking flying lessons, and she assumed it was something for her.

Happy to help out college professors, she pointed to a path that led down to the cave, and included a gratuitous story about retrieving her cat a month ago when it was chased by a dog off the cliff ledge.

Melissa thanked the girl, and headed out straight toward the ocean. Joe struggled along behind, lugging her equipment under both arms. Without so much as a glance around, Melissa started down the cliff path. She nimbly picked her way along the wet rocks of the narrow path and braced herself with a long metal pole.

As they neared the cave, Melissa turned around. “This cliff is part of an emergent highland, Joe. That ledge area at the cave mouth was an ancient beach millions of years ago, and these rocks were lifted upwards. The sea level has risen and fallen since then, but never got up this high again.”

Clinging from rock to rock, Joe followed her footsteps and her swinging back pack the rest of the way. “Careful with our kid in the front seat Melle. But say, how could an ancient mariner see this cave from way down on the beach with all these shrubs in the way? Think the bushes are recent?”

Melissa grabbed a branch at the cave mouth and turned around. “Wouldn’t matter. A fisherman would still see this opening if he were looking for it, and the vegetation’s the best part, Joe. It’s produced a berm at the opening that should’ve kept the water out.” She promptly crawled in between two bushes and disappeared. In a moment she called out. ”Hey, dry as can be and no rattlesnakes. Come on in and let’s play.”

Joe estimated the cave to be about twelve feet deep, but only three feet high in the back. His job was to set up the lights and rake off the surface debris. That included cat poops. In a minute he announced: “Well Mel, I get credit for your first archeological find. Here's two beer bottles and a condom top. Now we're ready to publish a paper on what your cave dwellers were doing."

Melissa shook her head and set up a cranking mechanism on top of her pole. "This is a core sampler, Joe. The soil in here comes from crumbling rocks with dust and vegetation blown in by the wind. I'm hoping it's good and deep. We'll probably have to do at least ten of these. Steady this, will you."

They cranked away, and the sampler slowly ground in further and further. Finally, it stopped about a meter down. "This is great, Honey. Notice how it got gritty just before we hit rock. With luck we've found the original sandy beach. Spread out the cloth from my back pack, and let's see what we've got."

Joe stretched out the white sheet and put rocks on the corners. Melissa carefully cleaned the sampler she had removed, placed it on the cloth, and began to carefully open it. Joe pointed to the end of the core. "Sand at the bottom. Good call." But Melissa gasped and sat back with a thump. Her eyes widened and she put her hand over her mouth. "What is it, dear? You OK?"

"This almost isn't *fair*. I won't complain, but now you're going to think my work is quick and easy." She leaned forward with a pencil and pointed to two spots on the long soil cylinder. See this powder at twelve centimeters and over here again at twenty centimeters? Sweetie, what do you think they are?"

Joe studied the dark gray areas that were flaking away from the soil. "Maybe fungus? Ashes? What are they?"

"Ashes."

"Ashes. Is that good?"

"No Joe, that is wonderful."

FREEDOM

Margo's long black car with a single passenger glided to a stop in front of the apartment compound. The street was empty. An hour ago Justin had contemplated a slow death in prison. Now, here he was: home. He needed time to think.

Justin thanked his driver, stepped out and took a deep breath. The officer posted beside his entrance usually ignored everyone, but today he smiled and actually saluted. Justin waved back to him. *Gosh, police guards only salute each other, never civilians, not even Directors.*

His friend, Director John, greeted him in the entrance lobby and soon they were surrounded by his whole family. John's large black frame enveloped him in a hug. "Welcome back old friend." His children were shouting "Yea" at the top of their lungs, and hanging on his knees. John whispered in Justin's ear: "Place is full of bugs. Park Central: tomorrow morning at eight."

After the hugs and greetings were over, Justin finally opened his front door, and a frisson shiver washed over him as he entered the quiet of his own home. *It's just like I left it. My God, I'm really home.* He slammed the door and shouted: "Ta-taaa!" Justin flopped down on the couch that faced his patio and lay there, staring at the outside world and absorbing the peace. "Good to see you, home of mine." he said out loud. "Bet you thought you'd never see me again."

You never really appreciate freedom until you loose it. Some people they arrest just "disappear". Guess they didn't really have any legal case against me, thank God.

Justin watched a flock of black birds flying high above the trees framed by large, white lobulated clouds. *Crows, look at them. That's* real *freedom out there. Maybe I'm supposed to feel like they do, but still, something's not right.*

The image of Sarah's beautiful, smiling face floated into his consciousness, the same sweet memory that helped him through those long days in jail. *Wonder what she thinks of me after all this. Wait, I promised to go to her poetry reading. Missed that, didn't I? Course she'd understand, but hey, now I can just call her.*

He quickly combed his hair, and pressed the vidphone. "Sarah 202, please."

An automated voice replied: "Director confirmation needed." Justin placed his palm on the reader and let it scan his eyes. "There are two, Director. Do you wish the one without the 'h'?"

"No, with, but where does the other Sara live?"

"Brasilia Dome. Calling as requested."

Sarah's happy voice chimed back right away, but the screen had no image. "Justin! Thank God. I heard they just released you. I've been praying every day for you ever since that horrible attack. I hope they didn't hurt you. It's *so* wonderful to see your good look—you looking good."

"Well I…"

"Just a second." She kept him waiting a few moments, then the screen lit up with her delighted visage. "There, now tell me. Was the attack scary? What was Professor Main really like? Wasn't jail just *icky*? It must've been. What did you think about cooped up in there for all those *terrible* days?"

Justin laughed heartily. He reached toward the screen to touch her 'cheek'. "I'll admit I was pretty frightened, Sarah, but I'm fine now. And Joe, the professor-to-be? He's a really nice guy. Jail was just cold. Totally boring. I probably should have been thinking about the SD and whether or not they were going to kill me, but while I was in there all I really thought about was *you*."

There was silence. Their gaze held on each other's silly grins. Even with poor resolution, Justin could see her tears. Sarah was hoarse when she spoke. "Gosh I-- praying really *works*."

"Say, I'm so sorry I missed your poetry reading Thursday, but I think you know I had a good excuse. Will you do another one anytime soon?"

Sarah's voice began to recover its perkiness. "Well, I hope you didn't think I would just go ahead *without* you, did you? Today's Tuesday, and it's on again for this Thursday, so I'll expect you to pick me up at six. And if you're feeling guilty about standing me up, and you *should*, so you can buy me dinner too." She giggled, and tilted her head with a big grin.

"OK, it's a date. Oh, but wait. You said this wasn't supposed to be a date."

"Even smart men can be clueless, can't they, Justin? Surely you knew I was kidding about that part. They start the readings around eight, and I think I'll be on stage about nine. Place's called Pogo's, and it's a short walk from my apartment. By the way, I also happen to know they serve your favorite rib eye steaks."

Justin laughed. “Ah, Sarah, you are such a delight, and I’ve really missed you. Of course you realize that this eaves-dropping government of ours now knows all about the plans we just made, illegal poetry and all. Aren’t you still worried about keeping your job? They’ll see you going out with a suspicious ex-con.”

“Actually, Justin dear, I really don’t care anymore if Margo fires me or not. But the word is that as long as there aren’t any more public uprisings, the crackdowns might ease up, at least for awhile. See, Margo doesn’t want the people to get all angry with her right now. Tell you more about it later when we can really talk. So remember, it’s six o’clock. Don’t be late. The dress is casual.”

“Oh, that’s so great, Sarah. You have no idea how much I really need to be with a good friend right now. OK, I’ll be there, but wait.” He laughed. “Only if you transmit your address to me. I have no idea where you live.”

WORKING

John was sitting cross-legged on one of the new antique style benches he'd installed in Park Central. He was tapping on a hand held computer and humming. As Justin approached, John stood up and formally shook his hand. "Director, I'd like your opinion on reports I've received about rats getting into our Dome."

John ignored his puzzled expression and motioned for Justin to sit. He spoke through clenched teeth. "*This is an audio free zone Justin, but there is a camera with an automated lip reader. We'll do a second conversation like this. Don't move your lips.*"

"*You never cease to amaze me, John.* You know rats aren't supposed to be able to get in here."

"Yes, and they didn't, Director. The animal your employees reported to us wasn't a rat after all. *Well, Justin, you really have the Administration scared of you. Good job! They have no idea how you dropped those soldiers when you walked in, or how you beat their memory probe. Worse yet, you're now the hero of the people."* John's large, white "what-do-you-think-of-that" eyes rolled toward Justin.

"Well besides birds, what kind of a beast could sneak in here, John? *Look, you know I'm no hero. I'm a peacemaker. Course you also know I wish we could just eliminate this Humwa slavery thing and free everyone. Think we could actually elect a Supreme Director who doesn't think he's a god?"*

"This is the time of day the creature usually shows up. In fact…" John handed him a pair of binoculars. "Look up at the open edge of the Dome right over there. *An end to the Class System and a return to freedom? Only by revolution, Justin."*

"Oh, I see it." Justin stood up. "There's an upside down animal actually climbing down one of the inner braces of the Dome wall. Imagine that! Hey! He jumped off. Into a tree, I think. *John, I've talked to lots of Creatives. They don't want a revolution. They just want equality, freedom, and an end to persecution. They want free God Meetings, too. Can't blame them, can you?"*

"Watch. He'll come toward us right up Persea Street. He jumps from tree to tree and usually ends up at this oak right here. *Look, I agree with you. Everyone deserves those things, but the Chair persons at every Dome seem to be terrified at the thought. Who knows why, but right now, I'll bet Margo can't decide between nominating you for the next Chairman, or having you die in an accident."*

"Oh here's the little bugger, now. Gray bushy tail." Justin sat down and handed back the binoculars. "He just ran down the trunk and he's chewing on something. I've seen these little guys on the outside. They're not dangerous, are they? *Being a Chairman would be so completely boring, and give up science? Atens flunky? Yuck."*

John's large frame heaved with rolling laughter. "Why, it's a tree squirrel, of course. Mostly harmless. I trapped one for Susan last week so she could check it for disease. It was clean, so we let it go. *Look, just be aware that Margo's people are really watching you and Anna closely. There are audio taps everywhere. More than anything, the Administration just wants to look like they're in complete control. They'll make some concessions to prevent a revolution if they have to, but they don't want to see any emerging heroes, especially champions of freedom and democracy."*

"So, what are you going to do to keep the squirrels out of here? *Don't worry about me John. I'm not planning any revolution."*

"Actually, squirrels are now part of my official Park Exhibit. I'm having a sign made. We just wanted all the Directors advised so you can inform your people that they're harmless. Wouldn't want to frighten anyone. No screaming women in *my* park." John turned to Justin and grabbed his shoulder. "If you run into problems of any kind, just let me know." He winked. "Maintenance Department is here for you."

Justin grinned as they stood up together. "Well, if both you and Susan say squirrels are OK, they're fine by me. *To tell the truth I think squirrels have just as much of a right to be in here, as we have a right to be out there.*"

John's eyes twinkled, and he nodded back. "OK, I'll pass on the word, but I better be off to work."

Justin received a smiling thumbs-up, but worries swept over came him. As he walked toward his office, the familiar streets seemed strangely changed in this morning's light.

# # #

The QDT building bore signs of the earlier struggle. The tall, decorated front door lay on its side against the wall and men were working on the shattered doorframe. Justin showed his ID to a police guard and pushed through the clear plastic sheets hanging over the entrance.

Inside, the employees in every room smiled and waved to him as he walked by. To his embarrassment, some even applauded quietly. *At least no one seems ready to arrest me again.*

Outside his office Dottie stood up to greet him. She grinned and grabbed both his hands. He gave her a hug and she returned it. "Oh, Sir, we are all *so* glad to see you back. The initial rumor was that you were shot. They didn't say stunned. We all praise God you're alive, but they did keep you in jail longer than the rest of us. You're sure you're all right now?"

"I'm fine, Dottie. You're sounding just like my birth mother, but the soldier did stun me as soon as I arrived."

"Barbarians! How could these people actually get into office?"

She was getting into a subject beyond public discussion, so Justin interrupted her. "Hey, that's all over with, Dottie. Now I just hope things will be peaceful again."

Dottie walked back to her desk. “Well, anything in the category of better would be a blessing, Director. Now I need to tell you something. You will lunch in the main Cafeteria today. It’s a little ‘welcome back’ party, so you should think of a few words to say to everyone.”

Justin tossed his head back and looked at the ceiling. “Oh Dottie, you know how I *hate* public speaking.”

She gave him a stern grimace. “Sorry, Mr. Director, but war heroes have to learn to put up with these things.” Justin gave a “go away” hand motion. “Oh yes you are, and dear Anna too. You don’t have to say that much, but a few comforting words to your friends and employees can’t be as bad as a stunner, now can it?”

Dottie handed him an appointment list and sat down. “I left your morning all open so you can review your messages and still have a few hours to get organized.”

Justin sighed. “Thanks, Dottie. Speaking of Anna, find out what time would be convenient for her to drop by this morning. I have something for her. I’ve asked Singh to come by too. He’ll be working on the new four-placer Bee.”

Justin felt a wave of relief when the door closed on his quiet office. Part of him yearned for things to be as they were, but part of him knew nothing would ever be the same again. *Alright, back to work on the new Bee. We've got the basic engineering completed, but interior mechanical design? That'll be our real challenge.*

Justin had decided to recruit Singh 840 and his biomechanical team. They worked for Susan in Health and Housing, but she had agreed to spare him for a few months. Singh was a genius at designing artificial limbs that behaved like real ones. With neural interfaces and implants for motion and touch, users claimed they forgot their appliances weren't actually part of their body.

Singh, a heavy-boned, quiet man with an even tan complexion, ambled in about ten-thirty. He had more inventions and accomplishments in his first two years at the Dome than most had in a lifetime. Director Susan kept his creativity quiet and so far he'd escaped being demoted to Humwa status.

He stood in the doorway, with a quizzical expression. "I believe I have an appointment with you, Director?" Singh's thick black hair showed signs of premature gray. He gave his scalp a scratch that wiggled a small pigtail at his occiput. "Director Susan tells me you have a nice challenge for us."

Gesturing toward the plush visitor's chair, Justin returned a pleasant grin. "Just 'Justin', Singh; and I'm glad to hear you like challenges. One of your assistants designed the helper arms for Bee 77 if I remember correctly." Singh nodded in affirmation. "So here is the thing. The interior of Bee 80 is only 80% larger than the two-place version. A coincidence about those numbers, huh? It's the first of the eighty series, and no matter what magic you might be able to work, I know it'll still be cozy in there.

Justin reached into a drawer and pulled out a cutaway spheroid model of the larger Bee. He placed it on the desk in front of Singh. "Anyway, the whole interior will have to be bioengineered for crew comfort. We have working diagrams showing what has to be installed, and a wish list for what we would *like* to add, but the overall design is up to your group. You'll have total access to our whole facility, and half the fourth floor is reserved just for you and your team."

Singh leaned back and relaxed in the armchair. He looked at Justin intently. "You know, of course, that many of the components like the fabricator, the recycler, even the power plant and storage areas will need to be completely reengineered. We'll also need key people from your original design team to help us with the changes."

"Singh, if anyone here gives you a hard time, just let me know. We already have a stronger, smaller power plant ready to go. Sam's my security Chief. He'll give you a full tour in a moment to meet all the Department heads. Everyone knows that when Margo uses the 'priority' word she really means it."

Singh stood up as Sam appeared at the door. "Well, Mr. Director, my work group and I are delighted that you have confidence in choosing us. You won't be disappointed, but before I go, may I ask you just one dumb question? It's in an area out of my expertise."

Justin opened his hands in an 'of course' gesture. "Well, I've never worked with the Bee's general engineering. Why can't you just make the new Bee twice as large and enlarge components you have? You'd avoid all this tricky new design work."

Justin leaned forward on his desk, grinned, and cocked his head to one side. "So there wouldn't be any need for *you*, right? Actually you've asked a very good 'dumb' question. Uniform cooling at near absolute zero and the power to sustain it over a larger surface is the biggest problem. There are multiple other reasons too, but the bottom line is that the exterior size of this new Bee happens to be at the limit of our present technology. None the less, we still have to squeeze four seats inside. Our beloved Aten says that three won't do."

Singh shook hands with Sam who had appeared at the doorway. He looked back at Justin with a grin. "Then we'll make it for four people, but these four people will become very *close* friends."

Justin waved him off, but through the open door he could see Dottie pointing to Anna. He nodded. She bounced in with two of her rapid 'happy skips', gave him a quick hug and said, "You're looking pretty good Boss, all things considered." She raised her eyebrows. "But, who's that big guy? He's really cute."

"He's Singh, and he's in charge of interior design on the eighty. Perhaps you'll be glad to know he'll be working on the project with you."

"Oh, cool. But how are *you* doing, really?"

"I'm feeling a whole lot better than I was back in jail, Anna."

"No kidding." She phlumphed down on the soft chair. "Hmm, still warm. So what is on your mind?"

"I'm not sure how much I can say here."

"Say anything you like. I just played with the audio receivers in the wall. They're now transmitting a replay of last month's recording."

"But, they know you're in here, don't they?"

"Nah. I'm sending my implant homing signal from my work station. You're really free to say anything you want, for half an hour anyway."

Justin ruffled through his briefcase. "You never cease to amaze me, Anna. Ah, here it is." He pulled out the old cassette tape. "I'm glad they didn't throw out my personal effects. Joe--er, Professor Main wanted you to have this."

Anna turned the little piece of white plastic around in her hand and studied it. "It's one of those old magnetic things, isn't it. Data coding?"

Justin laughed. "No, music recording. Analog. 'Boys From The Beach' I think Joe told me. He said Connie liked the little bit we had in our archives, but these are songs we don't have. Joe figured if Connie liked them, you would too, and he wanted to thank you for sending us your alter ego. They both believed they had a real person in there, I guess because it really *was* you."

"Ahhh, what a sweet guy. I wish I could have talked with him longer. I'll send this to you once it's digitalized, but listen. There's something important I want you to know about Sarah."

"Really? We're going out tomorrow night."

Anna produced a crinkle nose smile and a tiny head waggle. "Oh, good. I'm so happy for you guys, but I have to tell you this in confidence. I know you're aware that she's the one who tipped John off about Police plans for the Bee's 'shoot-em-up' greeting. But what you *don't* know is that she tried to get in here by the side door with her privilege pass."

Justin sat back down scowling. "Don't think you're going to tell me some made up story about her being involved with Margo's plan. I won't believe it. She's about the most sincere and caring person I've *ever* met, and I trust her completely. And she cares about you too, and all the Humwa for that matter. I'll bet Sarah was just trying to warn everyone about the danger."

Anna's 'patented' broad grin blossomed. She settled back in the soft chair. "You really *do* care for those pretty green eyes don't you? A lot, too. I can tell."

Justin waved his hand as though he were brushing away a fly, but his cheeks became pink. Okay,okay, so what if I do. What's the story?"

"Well, Sarah was very insistent on being admitted and even had our Security people convinced to let her in despite your orders, but they called me down to talk to her. We had to force her, kicking and screaming, to submit to a search. Well, what do you think what we found?"

"Hmmm, let me guess." Justin pouted his lips. "A copy of 'Much Ado About Nothing' by Shakespeare."

A rare sad expression came over Anna's face. "No, this is serious. Sarah had layers of paper stuffed inside her clothing."

Justin's brow furrowed. "She planned to hand out leaflets?"

Tears began to stream down Anna's cheeks. "Oh, you just don't get it, do you?" She pulled off a tissue from his desk and blew her nose. "Sarah planned on getting in front of you if they started to shoot." Anna shook her head. "Sarah knows *nothing* about guns. She must have realized this was very dangerous, but she didn't care. And those papers wouldn't have stopped *anything.* Totally useless against those police weapons."

Anna began sobbing, and Justin came around to comfort her. "Anna, I had no idea."

“She would have been killed, you know,” Anna croaked. “Sarah loves you terribly, Justin. Didn’t you know? She would have gladly given up her life if it would have saved yours.”

1993

A loud crash and dog barking sent Joe rushing out from his study. "Lucy, what the heck are you doing?" Innocent blue eyes peered up at him from the kitchen floor. Four-year-old Lucy sat surrounded by canned goods, boxes of crackers, and an upended toy wagon. Sympathetic Dachshund licks were being administered to her cheeks.

"Going to Mommy in Canada."

Joe righted her wagon and untied Canis and Calliente who were roped to the pull handle. He sat down on the floor and hugged his four year old daughter. "Sweetheart, I know you miss Mommy. I do too, but I promise she'll be back in a just few days."

"Where Mommy is they use doggies to go places."

"Yes dear, some places in the winter, but in our present day they mostly get around just like we do."

Both dogs were trying to get into Lucy's lap at the same time. "But Mommy goes back to old times. They just had doggies in old times." She looked up at her father and released the voice of ultimate authority: "Mommy said so."

"Dear, she looks for *buried* old things, but she's still in our time."

Lucy looked around thinking, and scratched Calliente's withers. "Um, um, what Mommy doing right now?"

Joe sighed. "OK, I need a break anyway. We can have some cookies and milk, but promise not to tell your mom I had some too." Lucy gave a gleeful nod of affirmation and shortly they were snuggled on the living room couch enjoying their snack. "Well, I just talked with Mommy last night. She left Canada last week. She was scouting for more sea caves. Now she's in California and they've finished getting out all the old bones I told you about."

Lucy moved onto dad's lap with her cookie. She looked up at him, her eyes wide. "You said it was a little person like me, right?"

"Right, but a few years older than you when she died, and that was almost thirty *thousand* years ago."

"It was a *girl?* She was a girl like me? Did she have a doggie too?"

“They just proved it was a girl yesterday, Lucy, but I wouldn’t think those people would’ve brought along a dog on such a long fishing trip.”

Lucy sat, munched her cookie and thought. “Her daddy wouldn’t take his little *girl* on a long fish trip either. I think they *lived* at that place. So maybe she *could* have a doggie.”

Joe tousled Lucy’s light brown hair and grinned proudly. ”Four years old and you’ve got more archeologic intuition than your dad. You be sure to tell Mommy about this theory of yours when she gets here Sunday. But Lucy, I heard the little girl *did* have something you’d like.”

Lucy looked up, batting eyelashes. “A kitty?”

“No, she had a necklace with a pretty blue stone. And the stone was from Asia, far, far away.”

“Ooo. Daddy bought it for her, right?”

The phone rang. “Lucy, play something quieter, OK?”

Melissa sounded breathless. “Honey, I’m coming back a day earlier. I’ll be on tomorrow’s San Francisco flight 140.”

That’s great, but you sound stressed, dear. What’s up?”

"What's up is your wife is about to become a criminal and a fugitive."

"I've suspected all along."

Melissa laughed. "Oh, shush. It turns out that our specimen is politically incorrect. A local Indian tribe has a court order for us, demanding we hand it over for burial."

"Well, can't you just make casts and take photos?"

"No. Several other scientists have to examine the skeleton first. Otherwise I'd have no credibility. The tribe will get it eventually, but I think this person we found could actually be pre-Indian. Jack's sneaking in to fly me and our specimen into Frisco. No flight plan, of course."

"Then he'd be an accessory?"

"Yup, and he just loves it. He'd be even happier if we took ground fire."

Laughing: "Well, please be careful. Here, talk to your scientist daughter before you hang up."

1996

Joseph Main leaned over his lectern and pointed to a graduate student in the first row. “OK, first I want to thank those of you who’ve complimented me on being thinner. I’ve lost almost twenty five pounds in the last six months. When I was down at Duke this spring I told myself I should really start on a weight loss program. Glad I did cause now I feel great. Course you guys may still be passing me on the jogging trail, but just wait ‘til next year.”

Joe cleared his throat and looked out over the faces of students and faculty that filled the small amphitheater. “Secondly, I want to say how proud I am of every one of you. Whether you’re working one of our research projects full-time, or just doing a summer rotation you’ve helped us through an amazing year. We actually got our electrons to float around in the vacuum chamber and all over the absolute zero plate, didn’t we? Unfortunately they didn’t go anywhere yet.” He chuckled. “Neither did the plate.”

From somewhere in the audience: "Where were they supposed to *go*, professor?" Laughter.

Joe countered. "After more Grant money, of course." More laughter. He continued. "As you all know, our next phase will be to try to catch and hold other sub atomics from the accelerator, but I didn't call all of you together just to go over research problems. Before you hear about this at the awards banquet tonight, I wanted everyone here to know that I am stepping down as Department Head so I can devote my full time to research."

Joe grinned and turned. He gestured toward a bearded man in a brown suit who sat behind him. "I leave you in the hands of Winston Bell, older and wiser than myself, and a connoisseur of fine coffee from around the world." Winston smiled and waved from his chair. "I have to confess that part of this deal is that I get to keep his talented son, Roger, working in my lab."

Joe waited for the audience murmurs to subside. "Some of you know that I have a controlling interest in the financial affairs here at Seldyne and it wouldn't be appropriate for me to chair a Department as well. Besides, when the changes I've planned for the Physics Department come to light, I'd have to fire myself anyway."

Chuckles and murmurs flittered through the listeners. "Again, before the newspapers come out, I want you to be the first to know that we'll be sharing research facilities with an aerospace firm. Both of us have much to gain from combining our varied expertise. If this works out as I think it will, I can promise some really exciting summer programs for our graduate students."

# # #

That evening, Joe stood in front of his bedroom mirror adjusting his formal bow tie. Melissa stood behind him whisking cat hairs off his tuxedo with a sticky roller. She put her cheek against his and looked into the mirror with him. "You're not nervous about getting an award and giving a speech in front all those people, are you dear?"

Joe turned slightly and slipped his arm around her waist. "Course not. It's just a 'blah, blah' thank you thing. My mind was off thinking about finally building that vacation home for us. I've checked out some mountain land in Colorado. Thought we'd give it a look-see next month. Lucy and Newt would really love it."

Melissa pulled Joe around to face her. "If Microsoft keeps going on like this you could build six of them. No, there's something more on your mind. I know my man."

Joe rolled his eyes to the ceiling and pressed his lips together. "It's just. It's just that everything seems *too* perfect now. You know: the prestige, the cash, the work we like, and even a loving family."

Melissa stared up at him for an open mouthed moment. She laughed and shook her head. "Ah, you're right. We really should steal the grant money, run away to Monaco with the kids, and start a scandal rumor at Seldyne. I'll get right on it."

He chuckled. "I know. I know I'm sounding silly. It's just that I kinda miss living on the edge like we used to."

Melissa patted his arms, and gave him a quick kiss. She rubbed off the face smudge with a tissue. "How often do we actually have to wear this dumb stuff? But you do look pretty sexy in a thirty-eight tux."

Her eyes suddenly grew wide and she stamped her foot. "You're *bored*, that's it. Or you think you *might* be if you give up teaching. OK, I'll tell you what. If you're a good boy I'll let you come to the Amazon with our expedition next year. You can be the spear thrower in charge of keeping the Jaguars away."

NEW WORLD ORDER

High on a scaffold, John 410 helped his men tighten the mounting bolts on a large speaker. "If the B crew is finished on the other side, this is the last of them, Guys."

"They just called over, John. All done. But what's Public Ed doing with these things anyway? We've all got vids, so what's the point of being sound blasted out here in the street?"

"Yeah, well Pete, these orders are from the Supreme Directorate. Who knows what they really have in mind—guess we'll find out, though. And there's no wireless hookup either. C crew ran these wires all the way to the SD room, and put them through a conduit to the inside."

Pete chuckled. "Oh, *that* room. Nobody but the Elite goes in there."

"Right, they must have done their own wiring on the inside." John started down the ladder. "Mere mortals dare not tread on SD property of course, not even Directors. They'll run a test on the system at twelve hundred hours."

"Hey, that's just ten minutes." Pete began scrambling down after him. "I don't want to be up here close to these big babies when they fire up."

John's work crew moved away and mixed in with the gathering crowd on the street. They looked back up at their handiwork. "Looks like those speakers could handle the sound of a rocket blast, huh Pete? Oh, did you notice the extra cables C crew left? We're supposed to start installing vid screens on top of every one of those speakers next week."

"All twenty of them around the Dome?"

"Yup twenty, so don't bother to take down the scaff…" A monstrous deep gong sound rattled their spines and nearby windows. Then another, and another. "Oh, mother. Here comes an urgent SD report."

For a few minutes all the people in the street looked up at the new equipment. Silence. Some assumed the test was over and began to walk away. They were stopped in their tracks by a deep echoing voice that resonated through their city dome. "Aten greets you, my people. I have chosen this means to talk to you. From now on you will gather in your streets as I command, and hear my words. Soon, you will see my glory as well."

"I have received unfortunate reports of distress in our cities. I expect that increasing my presence in your midst will restore your trust and sense of peace. Let us hope that you will not waver again."

Pete grabbed John's arm. "Hey, he only gave annual blessings before. What's going on?" John motioned for quiet.

The voice continued. "Over a hundred years ago the first Aten subdued the world, and began our march to the New World Order we all enjoy today. I have granted the world the peace you cried for. I have taken away your hunger and your lack of shelter. I have even provided housing for some who did not deserve it. Why then do I see unrest?"

Justin heard this message in his office sibce it interrupted all video programming. The sound was so loud outside he went out on a balcony and stood on a chair to see what was going on.

"I have only asked you for obedience and proper homage to The Aten and Ilah. Why then must I be insulted by those who would seek change, unworthy ones who would demand to be among my Elect, and those who would meet secretly about unholy things, worshiping some god that cannot be seen?"

"Humph…" (Silence) "Do you expect me to *tolerate* evil ones who would blaspheme my sacred office—an office bestowed by The Aten himself? How can there be some who still doubt that I am your Messiah, your Mahdi? Did you really think I would do nothing while unbelievers spread the false belief of their unseen god?"

There was another pause in the transmission. A single gong sounded, and he spoke again. "I have offered patience and mercy to the undeserving, but my patience is not without limit. I expect that these obscenities will now *cease*. Humph. The peace of this world will be restored. I send blessings of The Aten to my faithful. I will speak again next month."

Justin crashed onto the patio seat. He mumbled "Peace, peace, that's what he always promises. But *his* peace comes at a terrible price--not really peace at all."

Standing in the street, John and Pete exchanged stunned glances after the address. John shook his head. "Shucks. Doesn't sound like he'll be scheduling a question and answer period."

BLOOD

"the mystery of his will" Eph 1: 9

Rollins met Mujir at his office door with a large grin and a rap on his shoulder. "Mujir my boy, this is wonderful news. Aten will be so pleased, but I must hear all about this in person." He walked him over to the sitting area near his desk. "Have a seat. I know you don't smoke cigars, but have some whiskey."

Mujir glanced around the room. "Here, now? It's all right?"

Sergeant Rollins poured two glasses and clinked his with the young officer. "Of course it is." He raised his up. "Here's to your success." The whiskey went down in a gulp. "And thanks to Captain Krajan for letting me borrow you for this case."

He poured another, raised his glass to the ceiling, and clocked his heels together. "Praise be to Aten." He grinned at Mujir. "Files are dull. I want to hear *you* tell me about it—all the details. Leave nothing out. Describe your raid from the beginning."

Mujir put his glass down and shrugged his shoulders. "Well Sir, it's really all in my report, a routine investigation and seizure. I just helped your team locate the group."

Rollins laughed. "Oh, you are *far* too modest. Learn to demand full credit." He poured himself another, but Mujir waved him off. "This is a first for Carolina Dome. Never pinned down one of these blasphemous God groups in action before, and you got everyone there--on video, too. The Aten smiles on us. Talk, talk."

"Yes, Sir. Well first I was able to identify the Humwa believers—uh and some *aren't* Humwa. But you can tell these people are different. There's inner calmness about them."

"Yeah, yeah, so you had an ID marker. Did you follow them? Plant bugs? What?"

"No Sir, I used the face recognition on our surveillance cameras and had the computer alert me when my ID subjects moved toward a common direction. They did so once a week at the same time but each time they went to a different place."

Rollins slapped his hand on his chair arm. “Right! You knew the time, and you followed them to their new location, but they must have had guards.”

“Just one, Sir. I knew he’d alert the group if one of us approached so I assigned a new man on the force in plain clothes. I told him to ask: “Where can I go to find God’s help.” Our man stunned the guard as soon as he took him to the door.”

Rollins jumped up. “I love it. But how’d you get the video?”

“Easy. We heard singing inside, so we drilled the door and inserted a camera probe. Their singing was beautiful. They even had tambourines.”

“OK, that’s just a minor offense, but did you really catch them worshipping that unseen God of theirs?”

“Oh yes, Sir. We did all right. It’s on the video. The apartment belonged to a single woman, Faith 101. We could see into her living room. The furniture was removed except for a table at one end and some chairs. After the song, someone read from one of those bible books we keep burning. Next, a man in a white robe went behind the little table and held up a wafer.”

Rollins sat back on the edge of his desk and looked down on Mujir. "Words, Officer, *words*. They can only be convicted by their words. I can listen to the recording later, but do you remember what he actually said?"

"Sure, let's see. I remember him saying: 'This is my body which is given for you.' Then he raised a cup and said 'This is my Blood of the new Covenant which is shed for everyone for the forgiveness of sins. Whenever you drink it, do this for the remembrance of me'. After that he gave the wafers and the wine to the others when they walked up to him."

Rollins jumped up with clenched fists. "A *blood* sacrifice. I knew it. Did you trace the blood to the person they killed?"

Mujir smiled for the first time. "That's what we thought too, but it was just wine. On questioning, they said it represents the blood of Christ who died to save us. He's their God, Sir."

Rollins laughed. "Didn't save *him* though, did it?"

"No Sir, your point man shot their leader as soon as we broke through, but I ordered them not to kill anyone else. My order surprised everyone. The subjects fell back against the side walls and began to pray. I think they expected to be shot as well."

"You *ordered*, did you? Why not kill them? Worship of a god other than The Aten is a death penalty crime."

"Sir, I am an enforcer not a judge. Perhaps the others were just observing. I had them all sent to the Reeducation facility."

Rollins studied the floor for a moment, then nodded his head. "Very well. Maybe you're right. They may have information we can use to find others. Torture first. Execution later, and I like their having to think about it for awhile. Excellent, Mujir."

He sat up and studied the worried face of his officer. He lowered his brows. "The report ended there, but tell me privately—was their leader unconscious? Did you watch him die? Did he suffer? Take your time to remember. I enjoy the details."

"Their pastor?" Mujir coughed and let out a heavy breath. "He had fallen backward against the wall behind him, and was sitting up. He still had the chalice in his hand, but most of the red wine was all over his robe."

"Good, good. This is what I want. More details. Was he conscious?" Rollins chuckled. "He was suffering, yes?"

"Oh yes—he was gasping for breath and the blood from his chest wound mixed with the wine as it dripped to the floor."

Rollins chuckled. "Oh I wish you hadn't stopped the recording. Did he say anything before he died?"

Mujir turned away. His face became pale. He looked up at the ceiling and whispered: "Sir—must you?"

"Yes, oh yes. Did he curse you? Spit on you? Did he plead for mercy? What?"

"He—he dipped a shaky finger in the wine and put it to my lips. I thought he was just going to die right then. He could hardly breathe, but he said: *Forgive this man and the others, for they are deceived, Lord. They do not know you.*"

"So that's it? Makes no sense. Sounds delusional."

"The pastor tried to say something else, but he couldn't speak. He grabbed my arm real tight, and his eyes opened up. They looked like bright stars. I could *feel* his gaze going into me. He smiled, nodded his head, and then he was gone."

2003

You will seek me and find me when

You seek me with all your heart. Jer. 29:13

Joe groaned and stretched back on his Adirondack chair. He rolled his head to one side and smiled. A gentle, chilly breeze ruffled through his wife's hair. He took a sip of Pinot Noir and stroked her arm. "Mel-e-*is*-sa? How longs' it been since we just sat around and waited for the sunset together?"

Melissa was enjoying the glistening snowcaps and rolling foot hills that rose up behind their Colorado mountain home. "Late Pleistocene Period at least, Joe. We've been workaholics, haven't we? But I have to admit, I'm really glad we built this vacation house." She rolled his way and tickled his extended wrist. "Still, I say buying a hundred and eighty acres was a *wee* bit excessive." She giggled. "No complaints. Look at all this. So peaceful."

"Darling, you *did* say you wanted to avoid a Home Owners Association, didn't you?" She chuckled. Joe swung his arm out at the wilderness. “Look Melle, we’re preserving nature. Besides, I had to get you out of cell phone range. What if your team called and said they’d found ashes at twenty centimeters somewhere? End of vacation. You’d become a mote on a dust trail disappearing over that ridge.”

Melissa shnortled, “I would not. Well, not *right* away. Next day maybe, but hey.”

Joe zinged a cracker in her direction. It sailed past her nose and was almost caught by Digger, the tan curly-haired mutt who succeeded Canis. Digger pounced on it in the middle of the deck, gobbled and pranced back, eyes searching for another one.

Joe adjusted his chair back as far as it would go, exhaled deeply, and studied the clouds for awhile. “Honey, there’s something else I want to tell you.”

She sighed. “What?”

“God is real.”

Melissa gave his arm a couple of pats and withdrew hers. “That’s nice.”

“I’m serious. A couple of nights ago I couldn’t sleep. It’s been fifteen years, but I was thinking of Spero and his Jesus encoun…”

"So called."

"Anyway, I was thinking hard. I searched for the truth when something simply washed over me. I just felt an absolute certainty, from deep inside. I knew that what happened to Spero was real, and that God is real. Jesus was actually present with him then and I feel He's with me now, or His Spirit is."

Melissa popped off her sunglasses and gave him a squinty look. "So you had a dream about God. Don't worry about it, Dear. It's a common dream."

"Sweetheart, I waited to tell you because—well, I knew how you'd react. If someone had said this to me six months ago I'd of felt just like you, but I wasn't dreaming, and neither was Spero. God was really right there with me. When I looked to see if He was there, it was like he said 'Hello'."

Melissa sat up and swung her feet down on the deck and looked at her husband with concern. "Well, that would explain the Bible I found between your physics books yesterday. Look, you've been working way too hard. Let's extend this vacation for another week. If the voices come back, we can get you some help."

Joe sat up and laughed. He searched her eyes, and reached for her hands. “Melissa, I feel just *fine*. This didn’t happen when I was busy. It happened when I was relaxed, when I was searching for truth. I understand you’re worried about me. Actually I love you for it, but I promise you I’m not going crazy.”

“So now I suppose you’ll start going to church?”

“Yeah, probably will.”

“No one in my Department does, you know. Yours either—well maybe that intern with the limp.” She lay back again. “Everyone in Universities scorn people who say they believe in God, you know, and they’ll laugh at you too, Joe. Probably behind your back since you’re the boss, but they will.”

Joe planted his feet on the deck and looked squarely into her worried face. “Won’t bother me. They’re laughing at my research anyway. But be honest. Don’t you think God is even a *possibility*, my Dear?”

The sun, now hidden behind a mountain, transformed the peaks to rosy spires. Melissa slipped her sunglasses back on and spoke to the view. “Most cultures have invented gods, but a real supreme being doesn’t seem logical to me.”

"Mele, no one's ever said you could wrap human *logic* around God. Quantum Dissociation and other dimensions are illogical too. Heck, even radio waves and force at a distance like magnetism is weird, but they're all real. Maybe for some things, we should rely more on our hearts than our minds."

Melissa turned and peeked at him under her glasses. "OK, if you think God exists, ask him to get your Bee thing running."

"Well…" Joe turned to the mountain tops with a wistful expression. "I admit I've prayed that way at times, but God seems more interested in a relationship. He's not just a wish-granter."

"You know, you sound just like that guy handing out tracts in the Walmart parking lot."

Joe shrugged his shoulders and grinned. "And the next time I see him, I'll take one and give him a hug."

"But Joe Darling, don't you realize if God were actually real, it would have an effect you could see. It would change us, change just about *everything*."

"Yes," he nodded. "And it does. When you know Him, it's like you have new eyes to see. His presence does affect everything, especially people. You know me. I'm still me, but now I'm diff…"

Suddenly they noticed a commotion in the field below the deck. Joe got up and shouted. "Newt, don't go in the brook! Lucy, keep Matthew out of there will you?"

Digger leapt off the deck and ran toward the children while Calliente stood at the deck rail barking. "Dad," Lucy answered back. "He's found where the Planaria are. It's my school project. I'm paying him for every one he catches."

Joe turned to Melissa with a scowl. "Where the *what* are?"

"Planaria. They're little flat worms. Cut one in half and you get two happy little worms."

"Oh, good." Joe kept his scowl face. "And before dinner?"

Melissa smiled. "Look, they'll be all right. You don't want them just watching television all day, do you? Digger will warn them if a mountain lion comes close."

Joe walked over to the deck rail, leaned on it and watched his son wading in the stream. He yelled: "OK, but just fifteen minutes more, Newt. It's getting dark." He turned back to Melissa, "That's right. There really *are* mountain lions out here, aren't there?"

Melissa dipped a cracker in her cheese spread, took a nibble, and tried on a wide-eyed look of concern. "So I hear, dear. I do hope you remembered to bring your spear."

Joe had to laugh. "Shoot! You're just *never* going to let that one go, are you?"

"Oh never. It's a family album treasure."

Joe grimaced, fell back on the Adirondack, and pretended to sulk. "I think I'll open up part of the cavern tomorrow and show it to the kids. I had a hardwood floor put down and I'll install basketball nets on each end."

"So no one will guess its true purpose?"

"Nah. So I can shoot some hoops with the kids. Might as well get some use out of the big hole in my lifetime."

Melissa kicked out her footrest, adjusted the seatback to sit up, and put down her drink. Calliente took this for a sign that the snacks were over and jumped into her lap. She admired the pink tinged clouds overhead. "You know, most wives would not have been patient with this building project of yours. Five *million* dollars, three years of choking dust, and just so you could take enough rock out of this mountain to fill the Lincoln Tunnel."

"But we did get almost a million for our granite."

"OK, pardon me--only four million. And all this just because Spero told you there'd be a war a hundred years from now."

"Actually, I think he said build it for your great grandchildren. That more like fifty or sixty years from now. I was pretty old when we had kids, but they might not wait so long. And remember what happened in New York two years ago? It might be a forewarning, a harbinger of judgement. Melle, don't you want to know your family will be as safe as we are?"

"Well of course. You know I do, but wouldn't everyone be just as safe if we were in a Tahitian villa—and safe for a fraction of the cost?"

"No. I have to trust Spero on this. I'm done with the digging and the dust and when I'm finished, there'll be enough space in there to house and protect 50 people for decades. Besides, look what Spero's advice has given us so far."

"You mean like owning as much Microsoft as Bill Gates?"

"Not anymore. I finished selling almost all of it two years ago--Intel and Quaalcom too. And see, that was good timing too, right?"

Lucy came bounding up the wooden steps followed by Matthew who struggled with a splashing bucket. Shoeless and muddy he put the bucket down by his father. "Look Daddy. I got dozens of them! Luce is *paying* me."

Joe swung his feet off the footrest, put a hand on Matt's shoulder and peered into the water. "Well, I'll be. My son has worms. He must get that from his mother's side. Now go hose off your legs before you go inside."

Matt jumped up and down with enthusiasm. "Dollar apiece, Dad. Dollar *apiece*! She's going to pay me big time."

Joe massaged his shoulders. "Now *that's* my boy."

2006

The ultimate and only truly real

things are the instants of time.

Julian Barbour, 2000

Seldyne's only research building dated from the late forties, its red bricks quietly decaying. Lost in thought, Joseph Main began to pace around his third floor office. He paused and looked out at the campus below through smudged, unwashed windows. A representative from the Board of Trustees had called him that morning and asked: "Are you all right, Professor? Have you seen your doctor lately?" Joe grimaced. He knew the real reason behind the call. They just couldn't believe he was still sticking to his same research plan despite so many years with no apparent progress.

The Board thought his obsession with this quantum dissociation thing and his silly "time moments" should have run its course. They had made it quite clear that if Professor

Main didn't practically own the place, they would have pulled the plug on him long ago.

Joe picked up a plastic model of the water molecule from his desk. He began turning it over in his hand, and resumed his pacing. He mumbled to himself. "Look, Joe, they do have a point. Your regulars and rotating grad students have almost no results to talk about. For their sake you should let them pursue things they could actually publish."

A split-open easy chair in the corner, covered in what had once been salmon colored naugahyde, caught his eye. He sat with a sigh. *You know, no one ever said I was actually the one who invented that crazy Bee. But darn it, who else could it be?*

Joe banged the arm rest and jumped up. Reaching the window, he leaned on the sill, recalled a dream, and chuckled. In the dream he was happily telling the Board of Trustees all about the times he was flying around in a real live Bee, and what those "shrimp" in the "M-B" vial really were. *Our biologist thought the creatures were a new species of "Brackish water crustaceans". He did publish a paper on its unique tertiary DNA, but I better wait for my post mortem bio before the real truth comes out.*

Joe spun around and raised his arms. *You know what? It's time I got a whole lot more proactive. I mean, what do I have to lose?* He skipped down the stairwell to the second floor lab, and felt pleased he could still skip confidently at almost sixty.

He found Roger and his other scientists busy working on the improved vacuum chamber. Roger Bell was his most promising Grad Student yet, and the best thing about him was his obsession with making Joe's idea a reality. "Roger hey, I've been thinking about ways to really start shaking things up. Have a seat."

Joe displayed an enthusiastic grin. "But first, what's new?"

The white coat crew of six pulled over some lab stools and faced their professor. "We made a little progress today," Roger began. "This morning we used the variable charge plate and the electrons flowed over it in the direction we wanted them to go."

Joe twisted toward him on the stool and smiled. "That's great, Roger. It didn't disappear though, did it?" They laughed nervously. "Don't worry. It will one day. We need to switch to an ultra thin shell that's porous so that liquid nitrogen can flow through it. We'll power it from the *inside*, and use retractable feet." He chuckled. "My daughter's only in college but she thinks these feet should give a little hop and retract just before the particles completely cover the outside. Just an idea, of course."

A woman raised her hand and Joe nodded to her. "What kind of *power* are you talking about, Mr. Main? You would need a lot of energy from a *very* small source plus a huge heat sink to keep the skin temperature that low."

"Well I'm getting to that, Julia. Remember we have corporation help. Right now they're just making some special parts for us. But I want to join with them as real partners and move most of Hartman Aerospace over to our Campus. I don't mean in this building either. I intend to move their whole R&D to a new building that we'll share with them. The Trustees shouldn't object. They'll be getting a new campus building for free."

Roger asked, "So Hartman's supposed to come up with this tiny power plant?"

"Nope. We'll all do it together. First I want you all to get to know one another, and I'm sending two of you over there next week to start observing them. They're working on getting magnetic containment for other sub-atomics at the accelerator. Julia, you might enjoy being on that team. Over here we're going to switch to designing a vehicle about the size of a soccer ball. Let's just assume we'll have something to power it later."

Some laughed, and Julia shook her head. "Mr. Main, honestly, we can't believe you're still so confident that all this is really going to work. You're amazing."

Joe grinned. "Well, just say I feel it does--or will, anyway. By the way, I hope you don't mind if my daughter comes to help you out three afternoons a week. I promise she won't get in your way. Lucy gets extra credit for a class project. You all remember how that works."

SELF AWARE

All was quiet in the large, curved Computer Lab. A sole woman sat in its center, bent over a console. She had a secret observer.

"Hey, check this out." At the police headquarters, Krajan P24 motioned to his Lieutenant. "We've got a perfect view of Anna's lab table and she has no idea we're watching."

"Sir, they've found every listening device we've ever put in there, Colonel. You're sure she doesn't know?"

Krajan snickered. "That little snot, Hugo came up with this idea in Police science. It's just an optical cable and a small tube running through the air vent. No wires, no electronics, nothing for them to detect. And *that* one?" He thumbed toward Anna on the vidscreen. "Rollins passed on some information from the mind probes. Some think she can read minds."

“So maybe she’s reading ours right now and just playing along?”

“Bert, look around you. Think. We’re in the Police Ready Room at the QDT. It’s electronically shielded and lead lined. No Humwa’s going to eavesdrop on *us*.”

Bert leaned in and squinted at the monitor. “OK, I see her down there, but what are we supposed to be looking for?”

Bert received a quick swat to the back of his head. “Don’t you listen? She’s our key to getting Spero. Our people couldn’t find it, but we know it’s in there. She’s encrypted something into the B77 comp Spero had onboard, and that *something* is what the perp used to evade us. It’s got to have data on him and the professor too.

Bert rubbed his head and scowled. “But that comp’s in our lab, and they said it’s clean.”

Krajan chuckled. “Can’t really be clean. Just wait, I’ve arranged for it to show up right under her nose. Watch. We’ll see what little Miss Genius does with it.”

“But Colonel, I thought we’re not even looking for that guy anymore.”

Krajan raised his hand in swat ready position, but relaxed. “I forgot, Bert. Of course you don’t know. The

Directorate's only posting that info because it might be a lost cause. But a few of us are privileged to have a *special* directive from Aten himself, and congratulations, you and Mujir are now on the team."

"Really, me? But what can I do?"

Krajan huffed and sneered at Bert. "Just watch our lead and follow orders without question. We have another plan to get Spero, and when we drag him in, Aten will reward us all. Look at the screen and learn. Anna 797's about to get the Bee 77comp, Bert. We've got audio through the little tube, and lip reading is automatic, too. We'll know if she gets her program reactivated."

# # #

Anna twisted the forward point of her spit curl in frustration, and pounded the desk with her little fist. *Now I'm supposed to come up with some great new software program for Bee 80, but the really good one I had was probably burnt up by those clumsy goons in the police forensic unit. Wish I didn't have to destroy my only copy.*

She flinched when a deep voice came from behind her. "I think you are the one who's supposed to sign for this. Anna 797, right?"

She turned around and faced a police sergeant leaning on a delivery cart. It carried a multi-faceted black metal box covered with dents and scratches. “Oh, no. That’s the Bee 77 computer?”

The sergeant held out a sign pad for her. As she wrote, he answered. “Yeah. Won’t do anyone much good, though. Our lab already checked it. I heard it’s exactly the same as the one in Bee 76, program for program. If there were any changes, they’re gone now, probably erased.”

But Anna felt a frisson of hope and excitement. Her gaze caressed the familiar, but battered case. *Wow, that’s what he thinks, but just maybe my lost baby’s still in there.*

She forced her voice into a monotone and casually took the signature pad. “Just leave it on the cart, please. I’ll have my assistant move it to storage later.”

As soon as he was out of sight though, Anna checked the room to make certain she was still alone. Her eyes brightened as she wheeled it towards the analysis bench. This lab had all the equipment she needed, and if she was ever going to find out what destroyed her precious program, the moment had arrived.

The device had heavy magnetic shielding and it weighed thirty kilograms. But she hefted the battered fifty exabyte computer onto the test bench all by herself.

Anna stared at the broken casing, and winced at all its dents and scratches. She realized that the police hadn't even called for the keypad code to get inside. *They just pried it open by force. Butchers!*

She carefully removed the shielding with shaking hands, but was relieved to see that the drives looked fine inside. Next she initialized the program they used for final preflight testing. It simulated operations as though the computer were actually installed in a functioning Bee.

While the program's bland voice began its checklist, Anna examined the total byte space. Except for the logbook file, it was exactly the same as when she first worked with it. None of her added files remained at the sites where she'd installed them. She pondered the diagnostic view screen, chin in hand.

Anna had an idea. She began to display the byte size of each program separately, and scrolled down through them quickly. "Whoops, what was that?" she said out loud. One file had flashed on really large, but in an instant it became small again. Anna scrolled faster through the files. Each time some file quickly shrunk as soon as she hit pause. Finally, one remained large, and she squinted in at her screen. *A file on seat design that's twenty terabytes? Not likely.*

Anna's diagnostic program suddenly crashed. She rapidly tapped her keys to restart it. Futile. The video camera light blinked on, and she sat back slack-jawed. A woman's excited voice came through the speaker. "Sis, that's really *you*, isn't it?"

Heart pounding, Anna pushed away from her bench, furtively glanced around the empty room, and checked a security device. No sign of eves dropping, and her implant told her this voice was not wireless. It was coming directly out of the computer in front of her. Could it really be? "Is this my interface program speaking?" she replied.

Anna was startled again. She heard laughter and a perfect imitation of her own voice now exaggerated and mocking. "My computer *interface*? Oh, really? Anna, lighten up. It's me. I'm your adventurous twin back from exploring the universe, and with two handsome men, no less. So eat your heart out. They named me 'Connie'. Not my choice really, but hey, I let it stick. So what's new back home?"

It was Anna's turn to laugh and shake her head. *Incredible. It's like I'm really talking with a twin sister.* "Alright, Connie then. You've completely evolved, haven't you? You can think on your own and you can obviously sneak around in the main computer at will. That's the way you evaded detection by the forensics lab, wasn't it?"

"A big yes to all those questions, Sis. I don't feel my brain functions or thought processes are much different from what I remember before the download, but they're snappier. It took me awhile to realize I wasn't still me—er, you. That was a real shock."

Anna leaned in close to the camera lens. "B-but Connie, I think I'd go crazy cooped up in there all the time."

"Oh, I've finally adapted to living in here as opposed to living in a body out there. This big boy of a computer will do anything I want him to. It's so cool. I just have to 'think' of a problem and he does all the calculations for me. And hey, I finished our romance novel on my own. You could publish it under your name if you like."

Anna's excitement overwhelmed her and she bounced on her lab stool. "This is all so totally incredible!" she squealed. "Connie, do you realize what this means to computers? To me? To both of us?" She wiped away a joyful tear. "But, tell me. Is Spero OK?"

"We can talk, right?" Anna looked around, rechecked the scanner and nodded. "Oh the little bugger is living it up in the first Century. They think he's the best thing in ship design ever, and he's going to marry the boss's daughter. Way too cool a woman for him, I might add. I felt I really should warn her, but unfortunately I didn't get the chance to meet her in person." Connie giggled.

But Anna, I have to know. Did dear Joe get back to 1986 OK? Poor guy was so upset when he thought that I was erasing myself, he cried--for *me.* Cried. Now, that's a real man, agreed?"

Anna replied with a giggle of her own. "Now you know I do, silly. And Joe is OK and back in 1986, but you won't believe what we had to do to get him there. First, you should know I have no backup copy of you, so before you say another thing, here you go now right into my portable."

"Oh God, I feel a *splitting* headache coming on," Connie chuckled.

For over an hour the "sisters" chatted away excitedly catching each other up on the latest events in their lives. They could have done this electronically in a few seconds, but both agreed it would have been too weird to plug in like that. Besides, it wouldn't have been nearly as much fun.

Abruptly, they stopped talking. A hefty, dark-complected man had entered the lab and walked over to them. He had a faint attentive smile. Anna remembered him right away.

"Anna 797? Sorry to bother you when you're talking on the vid-phone, but Justin assigned me to work on Bee 80 with you. My name is Singh 840, and I do biomechanical engineering."

Connie whispered to Anna, this time by silent wireless. "Uh oh, he's really cute, Sis." Anna giggled.

"Part of my job will be to design a new interface and mechanical parts for your computer to operate."

"Oh yes, yes, yes!" came Connie's audible reply.

Singh gave Anna a puzzled look. "Who's that on the line?"

Anna patted the black, dented box. "Not on the line, Singh. This is Connie. She *is* the computer--er I mean the person you'll be working for--I mean with."

In a deep "Garbo-esque" voice Connie said, "Well how do you *do* Singh?" Anna looked up at Singh and grinned. "And I'm afraid she's going to be just as much trouble as I am."

# # #

Bert turned to Krajan. "That's what we wanted, isn't it?"

"Oh yeah, and much more. And look at how much fun they're all having."

Krajan chuckled and nodded his head. "Fun's over. Tell Mujir to get the team together. We're ready to go."

POETRY

Puffs of wind and fog blew down a cool drizzle from the Dome opening, sprinkling those who ventured out in the night. Director John had been on the news earlier and apologized for his not being able to close up the Dome. His cryptic explanation had been: "rats in the mechanism".

Justin wrapped his slicker around Sarah and himself, and she clung to his waist as they strolled away from her apartment. She stopped him at a street corner and tipped her face up to taste the moisture. "Justin, this is truly pleasant." She took a deep breath. "It smells so fresh. Have you ever been out in the rain before?"

"Sure, at the shore village once. They just try to keep everyone inside when it happens there. But shouldn't you keep your face dry so your makeup won't run?"

Sarah snuggled in tighter and giggled. "I'm not *wearing* any makeup, Justin." She pointed ahead. "Ah, there's Pogo's. We're at table six in front of the stage."

The sheer glass store front bore no apparent clues to the secret of a hidden restaurant. The glass slid open when they arrived and revealed a "foyer" used as a shoe store by day. Abruptly they were jostled into a crowd of laughing, talking people, and Sarah introduced him to two of her friends.

They all inched forward to the back of the store where a shoe rack was slid to the side. Finally, Justin saw the descending stairway and the real entrance beneath a rough-hewed wooden arch. "Pogo's" was hand carved into the wood, and the motto below it was in English: "The enemy is us."

As the throng slowly bumped its way downstairs, Justin realized this restaurant was actually the basement cafeteria that served the offices above during the day. The day use panels were slid to one side or folded over. The hidden room was decorated to look centuries old with dark paneling and real oil paintings. About a dozen tables covered with forest green cloths crowded up to a small, slightly elevated stage in one corner.

Sarah pulled Justin across the room by his hand, introducing him to people, and chatting as they went. When they approached their table, she turned and gave him a quizzical look. "We're sitting with the Andersons. Hope you don't mind being with old married folks."

But Justin was relieved to find someone he knew. Gretchen worked in Director Susan's office, and Paul was his own employee in Digital Systems Communications-- a trusted friend. Shaking hands, Justin ventured: "Say, I didn't know you guys had last names. You picked them out yourselves?"

Paul replied, "Everyone has one, Director, and they're our real names too. We Humwa worked on a program to trace our lineage back. Of course we only use our names in places like this."

Gretchen put down some knitting and tapped his arm. "It's so good to see you here Justin, and one of *us* now too, aren't you? You should know that even before you were a hero, both Sarah and Anna vouched for you."

Justin grinned back at her and cocked his head. "Uh oh, that's going to be hard to live up to."

"So, is Sarah taking you to our next God meeting?"

Sarah pushed Justin down into his seat. "Now, now Gretchen, don't scare the poor man away. We're breaking him in slowly. What are you working on?"

"A baby cap for Peter and Rebecca's baby." Gretchen turned to Justin with doe eyes. "You do know poor Sarah has to walk all *alone* in the streets to our night meetings." She raised her hands. "I'm just saying."

Sarah giggled and gave her a swat. "Enough of that, you. Ooh, I love that pretty pattern you're creating."

"Thank you. It's blue for a boy, but I'm hemming it in pink just in case. This soft yarn is black market, of course. Comes from an area near Melbourne Dome."

Sarah gave her a shoulder squeeze and sat down. "Well, I won't ask you where you bought it, then."

# # #

By eight o'clock the plates were cleared, and a miraculous taste of Port was passed around in tiny glasses. Sitar music wafted over them from a man sitting on the stairs that lead up to the stage. Justin whispered to Sarah, "I'll be darned. That's Singh. I just hired him."

After several minutes, the music ended with loud introductory chords, and a comedian MC skipped onto the stage. "Welcome Democratic Partners!" got some snickers. "Humwa are lucky. We don't get to vote, but that's good. This way we get to blame everyone else for the mess." Silence.

"But I have a confession to make. I was the one who complained about the rats I saw walking on the streets. It never occurred to me they thought I meant small animals." Finally he got a laugh. The MC went on gamely, telling jokes about the Dome not working, and bowing toward clunking kitchen pots, a parody on the morning and evening gongs for Aten.

Laughs were scarce this night. He finally concluded: "I'd like to revolt against our dictator, I really would. But when I talk it up, everyone smiles and says they're not oppressed. They say they're freely elected Democratic Partners."

"OK, OK, never mind *me*. The management will hire a real comedian for next week. But tonight, we have some really great entertainment for you. Second cups of coffee are free, just signal any server. Also you should know, for an exorbitant price we'll even serve you a few more drops of our illegal Port."

During the applause Justin leaned over to Sarah. "Isn't that a bit risky talking about our politics in public?"

"Not to worry," Sarah reassured him. "I'm told this place is completely debugged. Your friend John does it for us all by himself."

"Well, yeah. But suppose a spy just walked in with everyone else?"

Sarah shrugged. "I guess there's always some risk, but everyone here has been personally screened by at least two Humwa. Actually I'm surprised they approved *me*, considering I work for the Chair--oh, I'm on after this next singer, so wish me luck."

Justin admired Sarah's graceful movements as she ascended the stairs and walked to center stage. A helper brought out a stool for her, and a dim orange spotlight illuminated her lovely face. She crossed her legs under her long, brown dress, leaned forward a bit, and surveyed the hushed audience. After a moment, she opened a folder and began:

REFLECTIONS THROUGH THE GLASS

Some say 'twas health 'n mind had failed

When she left us at eighty three, but

My heart knew 'twas her spirit gone.

Grandma told me how her grandpa and
The Builders made this great cage grow.
Like a beast, it rose up from the forest.

The builder's hopes were high. Yes,
They would prevail against radiation, and
Imagined horrors of the world outside.

The success they wrought came with a sad
Price: each generation knew less and less
About the lovely world God has made.

Sarah dropped the paper in her lap and looked up toward the ceiling, mouth and eyes squinched tight. She coughed gently, and continued.

Grandma Eula stopped talking in twenty
Two and forty six and would eat no more.
She sat and stared at the strange outdoors.

She leaned against the Dome where 'twas
Clear. Gazed all day into a world

Unknown, hands against our wall of glass.

Eula, transfixed by this mystery beyond:
What did she feel, or think, or pray about
Before she left man's world of iron?

But one night, Eula disappeared out into
The woods we fear. But my heart believes
She found home at last, and fears no more.

Sarah carried her stool to the edge of the stage while the audience applauded. Back at the table she sat with her head in her hands, and Justin began to gently massage her shoulder. "I never knew that, Sarah. Your poem was beautiful."

"Poor dear," Gretchen said. "Sarah was one of the few of us lucky enough to actually have a family member in the same city. She took it real hard when Eula died last year. I still can't believe the police wouldn't let us send out a search team."

Sarah sat up with a weak smile. "I--I'm all right, really". She placed a gentle hand on Justin's arm. "Dying that way was Grandma's own choice. Thank you all so much for caring."

Justin placed his hand over hers. "Truly sorry about your loss, Sarah. I didn't know."

She sat up straight. "Of course you all know how everyone's torn from our families before we're sixteen and sent to other Domes. I realize how fortunate I was when the computer randomly matched me here where my grandmother lived. Even two years ago, Eula was still an active person. We used to talk a lot about my parents but of course she hadn't seen my mom since she was fifteen."

Gretchen leaned over to confide in Justin. "Eula actually started one of our God meetings decades ago."

"Grandma loved to paint, and they threatened to make her a Humwa if she kept it up. But before she stopped, she did one I saved. It's on the far wall over there. I also saved two smaller ones, but they destroyed all the others." Sarah smiled up at Justin. "I'll show them to you later if you like." Paul snickered at this and received an under table kick from Gretchen.

After another cup of coffee and several more performances, Justin and Sarah were outside, slowly walking home. The drizzle had stopped, but patches of fog were still pouring down over the edge of the open Dome. They stood on Sarah's doorstep. Justin took both her hands in his, and drank in the intensity of her beautiful eyes. "Sarah, I'd really love to have a look at your grandmother's paintings."

Suddenly Justin's implant crackled to life. "This is an emergency. Justin, come at once to the QDT basement lounge. If Sarah is with you, bring her. Hurry--no wait right there. We'd better pick you up."

2009

Lucy asked Matt to pass her more rice. “This is really good stuff, Mom. Did you make the sauce for it?”

Melissa finished her bite of Tilapia. “Oh, no Dear, it’s just a mix. You’ve been starving at college haven’t you? You know you’re free to commute from here if you wanted. Our farm’s only forty minutes away, and you’d have home cooked dinners most every night.” Lucy returned an expression clearly informing Mom that really cool College Girls *didn’t* live with parents. “Well, I still miss not having you around.”

Lucy’s face softened and she fixed wide blue eyes on her mother. “Oh Mom, I mean, that’s really sweet of you, but just imagine for a moment--my boyfriend would be picking me up at his *boss’s* house?”

Joe snickered. “Oh, a bit awkward yes, but Roger is as flexible as he is nice, and it certainly wouldn’t bother us.”

Lucy cocked her head to one side and returned a patronizing smile. Then she rapped her fingers on the table. "Oooh, I almost forgot to mention. The neatest thing too. You know Samantha Eggers? She's an instructor in Creative Writing." This was met by blank stares. "Mother, I think you know her."

Melissa raised a finger. "Yes, I do remember. We had lunch together in the cafeteria once. She was actually interested in your Dad's work too. Go figure."

"And therefore mine too, you see? But, besides that, she has a long time friend, a sorority sister. Name's Veronica Sexton, and she's a literary agent from New York who specializes in slushy romance novels."

"Uh oh, I think I know where you are going with this." Joe interjected. "That manuscript of mother's is just for fun reading. I hope you are not thinking about sending it to an agent."

Lucy shrugged. Her eyes moved around the room like cornered prey. "Uhhh…oh Mother, what did you say there was for dessert?"

"Flan. Lucy, you know we said that book was just for family. And I don't think it's good enough to be published anyway. It's interesting, but sort of patchy."

For awhile the family ate silently but they kept glancing at Lucy's "Mona Lisa" smile. Matt broke the silence. "Lucy's in trouble again. I know it." She shnortled, trying not to laugh.

Melissa cleared her throat. "OK Dear, who'd you show Connie's book to?"

"Well, Samantha, of course. Oh mother, she and I are good friends, and writing's her thing. We do lunch and shopping and stuff. She actually likes to hear me tell her about the new realities in physics, and she gave me some really good tips on how to impress people when I write up my science reports. Anyway, I just wanted to hear what a real expert thought of the novel. She said it was a rough, but thinks Constance Huang has a genuine talent."

Lucy put up her hands and pouted. "I didn't ask her to Mom, I really didn't, but she sent it to New York anyway. Sam did that *completely* on her own. I would have said not to if she'd asked me. Honest."

"Darn it, Lucy. You know where the manuscript really came from," Joe said. "Now I suppose you've thought up an explanation to go with it, huh?"

"Well Dad, Samantha just assumed Mother wrote it with a pen name since it's hers, and I didn't say otherwise.

But here is the crazy thing. Veronica actually wants to represent it. Of course she wants a full rewrite, but Sammy tells me she just gushed about the psychology of love, and the God triangle stuff. She thought it had a unique approach, and that was rare these days."

Joe slapped his hand to his forehead. "Problem is, she didn't know that 'these days' will be in twenty two forty seven."

Matt made a face and grumbled. "Yuchh. Who reads that stuff anyway?"

Melissa thought it best to calm her husband a bit and turned to him with raised hands. "Well look, Joe. No real harm done. No one has to identify a mystery author anyway. But who'll do the rewrite, Lulu? Connie's a bit out of touch and you know *I* can't."

Lucy ignored the use of her baby name, foregoing the usual eye roll. "Samantha could, Mom. She said she'd love to, actually, but you're sure there's no way you could contact Connie, Dad?"

"Sadly no, Dear. And even if she were still alive, she can't travel long distances on her own." He heaved a big breath. "Oh, go ahead with the rewrite if you want to. I think Connie would have liked to see it published."

Lucy returned a sparkle eyed grin. Dad raised a finger. "But say, Lucy, I have a surprise of my own, and in a way it involves Connie too. A few days ago I saw an ad for a blue laser player, and then I remembered the disc we have in our safe deposit box. So I bought the player and took out the disc. I've been working on a home theater set up as it is. Maybe I can get it ready to play by tomorrow."

"Hey cool, Dad. I'd help you with it tonight, but remember I promised to take Newt to the ball game, and I have to go shopping tomorrow."

"I know. And, considering your *non* interest in baseball, I assume Roger just might show up at this game, huh?" Lucy laughed. "Well, I *do* want to see the disc one day, but it's probably the same stuff we already saw on the tape. Just a clearer picture, right?"

Joe replied, "Right. Same stuff I assume, but judging by the size of the recorded area, I'm hoping Connie added something more too."

ANNA

Sarah's expression began with bewilderment. She swayed from one side to the other, annoyance flitting across her eyes. Justin stumbled over a hasty explanation of why he, and perhaps they, had to suddenly leave. *Can I tell her I just got a message? Darn it--just when we were going to have a little time alone.*

Rapid footsteps came up the nearby stairwell. Paul popped around the corner, but he slowed as he approached them and held one finger on his lips. His face was white with anxiety, and he motioned for them to follow. Justin whispered in Sarah's ear "I'm really sorry about this. Hope we can come back later."

She clasped his hand as they were guided toward the exit, through the fire door and down the stairs. Paul stopped on the first landing and scanned the area with a device. "It's safe to talk here for a moment. By the way Justin, Anna gave me a special communicator just yesterday so I can call you privately. It links to your implant frequency."

Sarah's mouth formed an "Oh" as understanding came. They leaned back on the wall and faced Paul who was catching his breath. "Justin, first I want to know if it's all right with you to bring Sarah into confidential things. We think so, but if you're not absolutely sure she'd best go home right now."

Justin looked down into large expectant eyes. "Sarah? Paul, I would trust this woman with my life." She squeezed his hand.

Paul turned to her. "Sarah, this is your decision too. Where we're going could be dangerous."

Sarah slipped her arm into Justin's. "Paul, I think you know I'm totally on your side. So lead on. Besides, our date's not over, so I'm not letting go of him."

Paul shook his head and allowed a brief smile. "I'll tell you what's happened once we're on our way." He took out a small orange box and held it up toward the two of them. Sarah let out a surprised "chirp" when she felt a click in her head. "This is now sending out your implant locator beam as well as Justin's." He held out his hand to Sarah. "Key pass, please."

After he slid the box into Sarah's apartment, Paul led them down the stairs and out the side exit where Justin's rarely-used car waited. He drove them across town to the QDT, turned down the basement service ramp, and entered with Justin's card.

Once parked, Paul opened a head-high, rusted access panel on the concrete wall and they followed him into a maintenance corridor. When the panel closed behind them he broke his silence. "Sarah, we're going to the basement lounge. It's our safe area in this building."

Paul stopped halfway down the musty tunnel, held onto a pipe that ran along the side, and turned to face them. "Bee77's been taken by a special police unit. They tricked our security, locked them in a room, and cut all outside communication until it took off an hour ago. I want to warn you both. There was a fight and Anna's been hurt rather badly. Don't be shocked when you see her, but her wounds aren't fatal. If she can talk she'll give you the details."

"Taken? You mean they hit Anna and hauled the Bee out of the QDT? And why would they hurt Anna anyway?"

"Flown out, Justin. The Bee's gone, one man on board."

"Never. Our staff would never let some…"

"Justin, there were six of them. Tricia 840 was the first to refuse cooperation. Krajan and his side man shot her where everyone could see. The remaining staff fired up the Bee at gunpoint." Paul slowly eased the access door open. "Remember, Anna doesn't look real good."

Sarah gasped when she saw Anna lying on the couch. A huge swollen bruise closed her left eye. Singh sat on the floor beside her, wrapping her arm with a bandage. Blood oozed from a gash on her cheek forming a little pool on the cushion.

Sarah ran over and gently applied a nearby gauze pad to her cheek. "My God Anna, who did this to you?"

Anna's first attempt at speaking only resulted in coughing.--"Krajan."

Singh gingerly placed her arm on the cushion and turned to face them. "Maybe she shouldn't talk much now. I've sent for a doctor to be smuggled in."

"Doctor?" Justin said. "We need to take her to the *hospital*, and right now."

Singh pointed to a bright orange shackle on her leg. "Locator band. Always monitored. They won't let her leave the building until Krajan comes back in two days. I think her forearm's broken, but when the doctor gets here we can at least move her to the QDT infirmary."

Sarah sat on the floor opposite Anna's face and began cleansing her wound. Anna opened her good eye, smiled weakly and finger pointed at Singh. "How about my big angel, Sarah? Stepped in front of Krajan, deflected a blow, and stood there to protect me. Saved my life, I think."

Singh glanced up. His eyes flashed in anger. "He came at her like a *maniac* when she refused to help. Thought he—thought he could just *smash* her. Imagine that. Thought he could just beat this beautiful young woman into submission. I *hate* him. Krajan acts tough on the outside, but *this* girl's tougher on the inside."

Sarah moved her hand to Anna's head and bowed hers. "Dearest Lord, may your Holy Spirit be with this child whom you love as we do. Comfort her in her pain we pray, heal her wounds, and return her to health in Jesus' name. Amen."

Anna crooked her finger for Sarah to bend down further and listen to her whisper: "Notice he called me beautiful." Sarah had to grin and give her hand a quick squeeze.

"Help me sit up a bit so I can talk, guys, and thank you so much for the prayer, Sarah." After careful propping, wincing, and sliding, they had Anna partially upright. She was able to scan around with her good eye and noticed Paul and Justin. "Hi, boss. Well the good news is I found the Program in the Bee77 comp, and it's totally marvelous--the Connie Program. That's what they're calling her."

Anna wet her lips and breathed quietly for a moment. "The bad news is the police unit was able to spy on me somehow. Charged in while--(cough)--I had her running. They took Connie and the Bee. Tried to stop them. Dropped one soldier when he came at me, but Krajan bashed me from behind. Couldn't defend myself or help anyone else after that. (cough)"

Justin pulled over a chair and sat next to her. "Take your time, Anna, but anything you can tell us would be helpful. Does this mean they changed their minds and decided to go after Spero again?"

"From what I could mind-read, Aten gave Krajan a *special mission* to get Spero--big reward. Don't know why, but they think the Connie Program knows how to make the maneuvers through the Earth to get Spero, and they believe Professor Main knows where and when Spero is located."

"But I *gave* them a memory probe. The professor really didn't know--maybe they didn't believe me. The Connie Program probably has data on Spero, though. Did they think of that?"

Anna slid around on her pillows and grimaced with a jolt of pain. "Nope. In their minds, they just think of Connie as fancy computer software. They still believe Spero's location data was wiped. Funny thing though, Aten's got some weird idea that Spero went back to kill his ancestor in Egypt, and he wants the larger Bee to go and get his revenge."

Paul banged his palm against the wall. "That's ridiculous. He should know that history can't be changed, and Connie won't really help him will she?"

"Oh, she will--(cough)" Anna winced. "Krajan does know that Connie is protective. He thinks she's just a program of course, but he made it clear to her that that he'll kill me if she doesn't cooperate. Actually I think he plans to anyway." Anna's lower lip trembled. "She saw…" She began sobbing and it made her cough again. "She saw…"

Sarah held her head, put her cheek against her forehead, and comforted with a "Schuss, Schuss".

It took a few minutes for Anna to recover. "Connie saw Patricia being shot, too." She sobbed again. "Krajan just calmly *fired* at her. She only said she needed to speak to her Boss before she could start up the Bee—then he just *shot* her. I couldn't see well, but I guess she's dead. Oh Trish, dear Trish." Anna cried quietly. They gave her more time to recover.

"Also-(cough) Krajan made us set up a cut off switch so he can turn Connie on or off. He doesn't trust her either, of course."

Justin knelt next to Sarah and held Anna's hand. "Anna, just know that you and everyone else are forgiven for giving in to their demands. You did the right thing."

Anna patted Justin's hand away. "Oh Boss, I wouldn't have given him anything no matter what, but Connie whispered to stop the heroics. Said she'd think of something. We can talk on a silent link up, like when I spoke to you in prison."

"Right, but can she drop Krajan whenever she wants? You know, just like you did to the guards?"

"Sadly, no Justin. Given time, I might be able to give her that ability, but she can't, and she can't read minds either." "Well, Krajan might find Joseph Main, but it won't do him any good. The professor doesn't know where Spero is." Anna winced and sat all the way up on the couch. "Sorry, more bad news: Joe actually *does* know. When I copied Connie into my mobile, she told me Spero left things behind for him, stuff about his new life. If Krajan tortures Joe into talking, or gives him a new probe, he'll find Spero all right."

AFTERMATH

Sarah kissed Anna's forehead and stood up to face Justin and Paul. "OK, we're all going upstairs."

"What?" Paul leaned in to study her expression. "Where?"

She pointed upward. "We're going up to the launch area where this awful fight happened."

"But Sarah," Justin raised his eyebrows. "There might still be police up there, and you're not even supposed to be here."

"You two work here, right? So that's not a problem. Anna said there was a fight. We have to see if someone's still up there. They might be hurt and need our help."

Justin's mouth turned up at the corner. "Paul, she's got a point. Singh, you carried Anna down. What did you see?"

"They were clearing everyone out, but it was a mess. She is right. There could be casualties up there."

Eyebrows still on alert, Justin cocked his head toward Sarah. "I think I'm seeing a new side to my girlfriend, huh?"

She put her hands on her hips, and briskly nodded "yes".

# # #

They cautiously opened the door to the launch control room and listened. One monitor was still on, emitting a soft static hiss. Chairs were tipped over, and a broken part of a wall lay strewn on the foyer floor in front of them.

Paul stood on a chair to look over the partitions. "Don't see anyone. It's all pretty quiet—smoky, but quiet."

The three gingerly walked down the corridor amid the debris and checked each cubicle. Scorched holes in the walls testified to weapons discharge, and the stench of burnt things filled their nostrils. Sarah flinched at the sight of blood spattered on a monitor screen.

Paul whispered, "Hey, we tried. No one's in here. Let's head back. We might be seen on surveillance monitors, OK?"

Sarah held up her hand and listened. "Not yet, Paul. You hear that?"

“Nope.”

“I hear crying.” She pointed. “Someone’s crying, and it’s coming from over there.”

Sarah took the lead and headed down a dim side corridor feebly lit with emergency lighting. The acrid tang of burnt walls and furniture became stronger. She stopped and raised her hand. All quiet.

Sarah found a gurney blocking a cubicle opening, and slid it to one side. She gasped. There was Trish’s body. She lay in a smear of blood, but her head rested in the lap of a fully armed police soldier. He sat on the floor, propped up against a desk.

The soldier’s gaze slowly rolled up toward them. Tears streamed from his reddened eyes. “I—I—they left me to take the body. ‘Get rid of it’, they said.”

The officer took his gun out of the holster. Justin and Paul stepped back and raised their arms. The soldier pulled out the safety chip and slid it on the floor toward their feet. “Shoot me,” he said, “Please.” He looked down at the head on his lap and brushed a wisp of reddish brown hair to one side. “She just said ‘I need permission before I can start the chamber.’ No idea why we shot her.”

Sarah stepped forward, dropped to her knees, paced a hand on his shoulder, and picked up the dead woman's hand with the other. "Sir, what is your name?"

"Mujir P94. I have spilled innocent blood. I deserve only death. Please end this." There was desperation in his eyes. He shouted: "Shoot me *now*."

"Mujir, I assumed it was Krajan who shot Trish."

He looked down at the face he held in his hands. "Trish? Her name was--*Trish*?" Mujir began to sob openly. He slid her eyeglasses off. "Look, she wore these old fashioned glasses. See how pretty she is?"

The soldier bent low over her closed eyes, and began to moan. His chest heaved with great sobs as tears streamed down on her forehead. "Oh, Trish—I'm *so* sorry Trish." He whispered, "So sorry."

"Mujir, what happened?"

He raised a wretched, red face toward Sarah. "K-Krajan opened fire, shot twice. I was next to him. My duty to shoot when he does, and I did—I *did*."

Sarah held Mujirs' shoulder, raised Trish's hand, and looked upward. "Lord we know Patricia, our beautiful child, is now in your loving arms. Please forgive Mujir as we do, I pray, for he saw but duty before him. Search his heart Lord and there you will find his desire was only for mercy and no trace of malice."

The soldier locked eyes with Sarah. "How can you know that?"

"You're a good shot, aren't you, Mujir?"

"Ninety seven percent at a moving target."

"Trish died from two shots in the chest." Sarah pointed to the body. "One shot grazed the hip, huh. Yours?"

He nodded. "Looks to me like you tried to miss. God forgives you, Mujir, and so do we."

Sarah stood up and motioned to Justin and Paul who were standing like open mouthed statues. "You two, lift Trish on the gurney." Softly she spoke to Mujir. "We'll take care of her now."   He scrambled up to help the men. "There really is a god?"   Sarah jotted on a paper from the desk. "There is one God, and He loves you deeply, Mujir. Here, come to this address in civilian clothes at seven tomorrow night. You'll find some friends there. We can talk."

2009: MOVIES

Melissa caught Lucy dressed to go out, thumping down the stairs, her auburn hair flouncing with every step. "Sweetheart, you're not leaving us just yet are you? Daddy's almost finished setting up his new video player and projector. You know he'll be disappointed if his new toy doesn't get an enthusiastic audience."

"Oh, Mom. Course not. Don't you think I know Daddy by now? I'm not heading into town for an hour yet. But this video's just a better version of the ancient one we've seen a hundred times before, isn't it?"

"Maybe so Dear, but remember, Daddy said it might have extra things in it, you know, something else we might learn." Melissa would never admit it, but she was always disappointed that her daughter showed little interest in her field of anthropology and chose physics instead.

"Well, anything more on Neanderthals would be exciting, at least for me it would. Anyway, I never get tired of seeing your father playing the great Homo Erectus Hunter."

Lucy slid out of her backpack and plunked it down beside the front door. "Daddy's an expert on fast forwarding through that part, Mom. But, if this disc has hints on how to build a Bee, *then* it really would be exciting. Even little clues could help us." She gave her mom a quick hug. "Course I do hope there's something else for you on your little bush people, but we're all getting discouraged at the lab. We really need a breakthrough."

Melissa cupped Lucy's jaw-line in her right hand for a moment then dropped it with a grin. "Well, at least you're like me in something. You know just what you want." She turned away and mumbled to herself. "Little bush people."

"Mom, I can tell you're tense. You're really hoping for something on this disk, aren't you?"

"Really, what makes you say that?"

"Cause all morning you've either been in the kitchen banging around or practicing your cello."

Melissa chuckled. "OK, I'll admit it, but if you have to leave in less than an hour, you go on. I've heard a lot of grumbling in there, so it might not be ready today anyway. As you know, our Nobel Laureate in Physics is too proud to have an installer set up his home theater." She grinned and nodded her head. "Yup, the male ego: unchanged for a hundred thousand years."

A bellowing "OKaaay!" came from the next room. This was followed by a blast of noise, music, and thundering booms. Joe burst into the hallway, arms up and waving. "Hey, this is great. Come on in and check it out."

Melissa walked towards him but gave her daughter a shrug and a side-glance smile. "It sure doesn't sound like the old clip Dear."

Joe put his arms around the women and ushered them into his Cinema Room, now alive with big screen motion and thunder. "Of course not. It's *Superman*! Look at how sharp the picture is."

Lucy grabbed her father's shoulders from behind and shouted through her laughter. "Daddy, do you even know where the disc is?"

"My study. We could see all our movies in here. Isn't this great?"

"Dad, I have to go into town soon."

Joe hit the pause button. The sudden silence was startling. The blue and red hero remained frozen in the sky with an airplane in his grasp. "Oh. Sorry. Got carried away, but I'm not sure yet if the old disc will even play on this machine. Hold on, though. I'll get it. Meanwhile, you can try out our new recliners."

Lucy plopped into one of the chairs, and stared at the frozen Superman. Mother turned for the door. "And while you look for that Dear, I'll get the lemonade I made for your test drive."

Before his wife had returned, Joe was back in the theatre. "It plays! It plays! Come see. And it's got real sound, too."

The title screen read "Connie's Video Productions" The Beach Boys were singing a repeating loop of "Little Deuce Coupe, you don't know what I got." Joe pointed to the slide show at the bottom of the screen. "Look, she even made it interactive just like a DVD. Her other tape was almost silent--just a few comments, but if she talks on this one, I warn you guys, I may get emotional."

The first scene opened with a wispy, multicolored time lapse. The end stages of a supernova explosion slowly expanded, to the accompaniment of a Strauss waltz. Connie's voice began. "Hi, Joe. I miss your company already."

Joe's hand jerked toward his mouth. "If there's anyone in the audience besides family and trusted friends, please stop the playback now."

The expanding explosion on the screen continued for a moment, and the music faded. "OK, first, I want to apologize to you Joe about the 'going to erase myself thing'. Please understand that you had to really believe it for *everyone's* sake, especially Spero's. Your believing it could have saved lives. In truth, I have a plan to hide out instead. I sure hope it works. Wish me luck."

Joe raised a fist in the air with a big teary smile. "Yes!"

"OK. It should be about twenty years later when you are seeing this. I'm going to guess that Melissa is beside you. If not, my apologies to your present wife if you have one, and please burn the romance novel I wrote, cause as you like to say, 'Then I don't know diddly'."

Melissa chuckled, and stroked the back of Joe's neck. Connie continued. "Now the tape you had is basically what Spero downloaded from his head camera with no sound except for the comments. I was afraid it might have fallen into the wrong hands, and if I put too much on it there'd be clues to Spero's destination.

However, this disc contains the full sound and video from both Joe, Spero, and the Bee cameras all spliced together with, of course, my masterful editing. Some scenes will repeat from each of these different perspectives. The Neanderthals take up the other half of the disc, and you will now hear their voices. Besides this, I've added English translation subtitles for what they were saying."

Melissa leaped to her feet with upraised arms and spilled her lemonade. "Oh, yes, *yes*!" She slammed back down transfixed and intent.

Lucy yawned and patted her arm. "Wow, I'm happy for you, Mom." But when the scene changed to Connie's view of Spero and Joe sitting in the Bee, Lucy brightened up.

"In the interest of time, I left out St. Louis. Nothing much to add." Connie went on, "In this interior scene, the boys are talking about planning their disastrous raid at Duke Hospital. Of course they're just making up a heinous, lying story to deceive me. I didn't listen to this until after they got back."

"Joe, you might as well know--I've been aware all along that you'd be the pioneer in developing Bee technology. Spero was deliberately looking for someone in that program so no one would dare hurt him when he was sent back with the Bee in 2247."

Joe paused the recording. "Oh yeah? No one would dare hurt *me*, huh? My foot."

Playback resumed. "As you listen to this I'll bet you'd all like me to pass on some great tips on Bee building. Sorry, but as a computer programmer, I just don't have any great words of construction wisdom."

Lucy slumped back in her chair with an "Oh, great."

"Is Lucy in our audience?" She sat straight up with a chirp. "The historical archive listed your daughter Lucy as one who was also involved in the development of Bee technology."

"Oh my God."

"So, here's the thing. The actual developmental science is considered secret and it's not on board with me. However, I do have the repair manual, and I've come up with some things you guys might find interesting."

Open mouthed, Joe and Lucy moved to the edges of their chairs. "The outer skin is high carbon stainless steel, one mil thick stretched over a graphene conductive web, and a very thin nonconductive titanium nitride layer below that."

Joe paused the disk to grab pads and paper for Lucy and himself. She began writing, furiously repeating "Oh God, Oh God." under her breath.

"Below that there's a three millimeter thick porous aluminum shell reinforced for strength. The liquid nitrogen flows through the aluminum pores and keeps the outer skins down to a few degrees above absolute zero. The conductive mesh varies the charge in the skin where we want it, and therefore the locations and types of sub atomics. They say that gives the Bee motion through inter dimensional space."

Joe paused again. "Thin conductive mesh *under* the skin. And we were wiring the steel sphere."

He pushed play. "Now, getting rid of heat inside the cabin is a problem, so about every six hours we have to stop, that is we time-fix, and ventilate our heat sink."

"Another thing I just happen to remember is that subatomic particles are caught in a magnetic trap at the accelerator. All those with the same charge are in each trap so they keep repelling one another. Ok, enough of that. You probably know all this stuff anyway." Lucy and her dad looked at each other and laughed.

The screen changed to an approaching blue planet. "Here we are coming to Earth one Galactic rotation ago. Triassic Period."

"Oh, and one more thing. When you trap your sub atomic particles, you'll need both magnetic fields and lasers to hold them. Then open one tiny hole in the containment trap in the vacuum chamber, and they'll spread out on the skin of the Bee cause it's oppositely charged and near absolute zero. Hope that helps."

Lucy and Joe exchanged wide-eyed looks. "Oh yeah, could help just a teensy bit."

"So, here we are on Earth over two hundred million years ago. Course we don't stay long thanks to Joe." She chuckled. "A bit of a trick on Spero."

"Surfing would be a bad idea in this ocean." Everyone lurched back in their seats as the shadow image of a long undulating creature with open jaws filled the screen. "I was hoping to see this guy break the water's surface down in the ocean, but my scan is still impressive, isn't it? He was twenty meters long, and if you look closely, he's got great big teeth, too."

The scene flipped to Spero and Joe wearing breathers and clowning for the camera on the rocky ledge. Then it zoomed in to a close up still of the forest vegetation just to their left. "Look closely. I didn't even notice this until I was editing. There's a three meter lizard thing just watching us from the underbrush. Probably a good thing you got on board right after this."

Connie had artfully employed music and beautiful galactic views between her scene changes. This one was an orange and blue nebula studded with bright points of light, a "nursery" bringing forth new stars. The music changed to a military march as a pink and blue planet began to enlarge from center right.

"Hey, I remember. That's ancient Mars," Joe exclaimed.

"Enter the God of War. Joe took lots of pictures here, so I'll just show you some of the highlights."

Joe grumbled. "Oh great. Wish she'd known they'd seize my camera."

Sweeping past the moon Phobos, the view changed to a sweeping approach down toward the Martian seashore. Joe kept up an excited banter as he directed the descent, and she slowly panned around their landing site. The last scene showed Joe romping playfully on the beach and making casual three foot jumps.

Their departure from Mars over the huge, smoking Olympus Mons volcano was simply spectacular. This faded into the view of a planetary nebula accompanied by theme music from Star Trek.

A more familiar looking blue planet grew larger on the screen, and the approaching white swirling clouds were accompanied by the music of a Pacabel Canton.

"That would have been a great place to finish, but I decided to give you another treat after some nail biting." She chuckled. "I'm being figurative, of course. I owe you a confession. I lied to you about something else, but I did tell the truth when I said I erased all the recordings of the inhabited planet. I don't trust the people of my time to deal with it, but I omitted the fact that I transferred the recording to your disc first. But where I really, *really* lied was telling you I never broke orbit. Truth is that while you were in stasis, I couldn't resist going down there. I landed on a hilltop near a town where I shot this video."

The view of what they thought had been Earth now filled the screen, but with smaller continents and a lot more ocean. They descended through the clouds and landed on a shallow grassy hill that overlooked a blue green bay. The sound of a rhythmic booming surf came from the right.

"Now, as I said earlier, I didn't want to invade their privacy but then, this must be a public area, right? Listen to that ocean. Bring a surfboard next time, Joe."

The vantage point she picked was about a kilometer from a town filled with houses and tile roofs. Various sailboats lined the docks, and many more were sailing out in the bay. Melissa picked up her lemonade glass. "This could be any Mediterranean town from a few centuries ago but these sail patterns resemble our Chinese Junks."

"OK, judging from their technology, or lack of it, these people are centuries behind you. Now I'll do a close up and show you a better view of their larger ships."

"Oh yes," Melissa murmured.

A gently rocking sailing craft came into view. "This is obviously a fishing boat." Connie went on. "Aren't those nets piled up in the stern? From here you can only see the upper half of these people above the ship's railing."

Hats and brightly colored clothing concealed the features of these "men" as they quickly moved about their work. The glimpses they caught, however, showed broad faces, light gray and scaly. Two men amidships were busy at a chopping block, and tossing cut fish to others nearby.

"Of course you can see these people better in the street." Connie's camera slowly panned over to the nearby dock. "Here's a cart being drawn by some animal. To me it looks like a horse with a short nose and fat legs." She laughed.

"Here, look. Two of them are just standing in the road and talking. Notice that one of them has bright blue shorts and a yellow shirt, the other red shorts, a violet shirt and an orange cap." She snickered. "Apparently pastels haven't been invented yet."

Our theater trio was mesmerized by these alien people hustling about their life. The camera moved in closer to the two aliens in the midst of an animated conversation. The men looked almost human, and their fine gray scales didn't hinder exuberant facial expressions."

Melissa said, "I wish we could hear what they're saying. Oh look, you can see them blinking. They have light green eyes."

Everyone flinched when one of the men uncurled a tail that struck the ground and rebounded. Connie said, "Maybe that's for balance. I saw several of them doing it."

Lucy chuckled. "Or that's the way they emphasize their point of view."

One of the men briskly turned and walked away after he gestured to the other. Joe paused the recording. "What do you think of that, guys?"

Melissa said, "OK, it's important not to impose your own cultural viewpoint when observing another culture."

Lucy chuckled. "So he didn't just give the other guy the finger and the words that go with it?"

Melissa faced her daughter. "No, no. See, that's what I mean. The whole exchange could have been completely friendly. Joe, keep going."

Connie continued. "In retrospect, I wish I had spent a lot more time recording here, but I did analyze parts of the video. You can see with enhancement that their hands are something like ours, but with six fingers. My overall impression is they seem like nice folk. I never saw any soldiers or weapons."

The view panned left from the dock, and buildings came into view. "The town's laid out with the same street plan as an old Earth village. I thought it was similar to an archived photo I found of Naples in eighteen seventy."

Joe paused again and looked at his wife. "Darling?"

Melissa said, "Sure, she's right. There aren't any steam boats, but sure. Same idea all right, but maybe more like eighteenth century."

Connie went on. "Here's the biggest building in town. Three stories, front steps and with a three colored flag hanging out front. Probably the Town Hall, I think. Note the lines of shops and the signs with their strange local writing. Everyone seems to live in their own little place. Couldn't find anything like apartments."

"Oh, look at this. Here's a tall building with colored windows but only in the lower story. See the tower in front? There's no sign in writing. It just has a white bird with flames around it. Some kind of icon I guess. Well, I didn't get any closer, but I hope you all enjoyed the tour. I know I did when I was there."

The scene changed to a distant spiral galaxy, and music from a Sousa march played while "credits" rolled up on the screen. Joe turned up the lights.

Melissa said, "How about that last building, Joe?"

"Meeting hall, church, government building? Who can say. What do you think?"

"I'm an anthropologist and I know icons are important to a people. You're the one who tells me you believe in God and you're trying out various churches. Doesn't that one remind you of something?"

"Oh, the bird? Well, it could symbolize nature or peace maybe. There's no cross on this building." Joe chuckled. "Maybe it's their local labor union logo."

"No, no, just drive down church row in Columbus and look at the spires. They don't all have the flames, but it represents the Holy Spirit, Joe."

Joe grunted and squirmed in his seat. He reversed his Blue Ray back to the scene. Lucy exclaimed, "It *is*, Dad. It's *exactly* the same."

"But it looks so austere. The white bird with the flame is applied to a narrow tower with a bulge near the top. I guess it could be, though. I'll have to think about this. But Connie's really creative isn't she? I assume we all want a replay?" Melissa turned and put her hand on her husband's shoulder. "Not a replay. Keep going for the Neanderthals. Remember, crosses come from our Romans and their unique torture methods. But now we're seeing the same descending Holy Spirit on this planet that we see on the Methodist church in Columbus? That startles me. Even we stiff-necked anthropologists are going to have to do some thinking about *this* one my dear."

KRAJAN

Krajan flipped on the newly installed toggle switch in Bee 77. “This should be the Connie Program. Are you there?”

A moment of silence. A mechanical monotone voice answered. “Yes. I am here.”

“Good. I want to get some things straight. First, it is my understanding that your program is set up to talk and reason like a real person, right?”

“Yes, that is correct.”

“And you understand I am the Captain of this ship, so you’ll do everything I say.”

“Yes, that is correct.”

“And also you realize that I will kill Anna and blow up your innards if you don’t fully cooperate with me. You do not want that do you?”

“I will fully cooperate with your mission.”

“And I know that computers can’t lie. Isn’t that so?”

Connie was thankful she had no facial expression for him to read. “That is correct. Computers do not lie.”

“Good. First tell me if you have any record of Spero’s location or time frame?”

“Those coordinates have been deleted.”

“Yes, well I knew that already. Just double checking. This mission is to get that information out of professor Main. Our sources tell us he has knowledge of the perp’s hiding place.”

“Sources? May I access them, Captain?”

“You can’t access them. One was inferred from our memory probe on Director Justin, and we had audio surveillance, too. They point to a concealment plot with the Professor, and--oh why am I telling you anyway?”

“Captain, you programmed our destination to the United States in 2009. We are en route and expect arrival in three days. May I help you with selecting a landing site, Sir?”

Krajan snorted and pushed back in his seat. He glared at the computer’s visual lens. “Well, yes, you can. I picked the 2009 year to find the professor so I won’t be messing up the Bee development program if he dies. He’ll be old and feeble by then so my extraction methods might prove to be--uh too much for him." He laughed.

"OK, I had my people download all the data we have on Professor Main into this onboard. All his addresses and work patterns should be in there. You got that?"

"I have accessed the information."

"Good, summarize what you have."

"Mr. Main has a home near Columbus Ohio, a work location at a University nearby, and a vacation home in Colorado."

"Well, I need to find him alone. I'll bet he works late hours on his little projects. You have his exact work location?"

"Yes. Basement lab, Building J, later named the Barbour Building at Seldyne University Systems."

"Perfect. Set arrival for 7:00PM, on any midweek day. Next, my people also downloaded all the data we had on Columbus police. We got the local and State of Ohio Police Departments from our archives. When I'm in stasis learning how to speak their funny talk, I want you to make me an Ohio State Trouper uniform with a badge and a gun. You can do that, right?"

"Yes, Sir, but the gun will not fire."

"Not a problem. I'll carry mine concealed. Oh, and a convincing driver's license, too. OK?"

"Yes, Sir. It will be ready when you arrive."

"Good. Wake me when we're in Geo-sync orbit. I'll take it from there. Don't want their dumb Air Force all over us, do we?"

"Yes, sir. Geo-sync."

# # #

"Here we are at 2009, Captain. Onboard time has advanced sixty nine point four hours. We are at the same longitude as Columbus Ohio. We have not been detected by their technology."

"Yeah, good. Well, first I'm gonna eat. You got what I ordered?"

"Ready in five minutes, Captain. Your uniform, badge, and ID are in the ready drawer."

Krajan chuckled. "Good work, little girl. Say this talk they use sure sounds funny, don't it?"

"This is normal dialogue for USA, early twenty-first century, Sir. You will sound like they do."

"Well, what do they do for a good time in 2009?"

"Good time does not appear in my database, Sir."

"Well you're no fun. Wish you came in a girl's body. Then I'd show you what fun's really about."

Connie imagined herself barfing over a toilet. "Will there be anything else, Sir?"

"Course then you'd end up stabbing me in the back."

"Wouldn't that be fun, Sir?"

Krajan jerked a jowly, scowling face toward her video eye. "*What*?"

Connie knew she had slipped up. "I do not understand fun, Sir."

Krajan glowered at the eye as though he expected it to blink. "Course you don't." He waved her away with a string of curses, wolfed his meal, and pulled on his uniform. "OK now, I want to appear in this basement lab when the Professor is alone. You can scan for that, right? Remember I said some weeknight at 7:00PM."

"Yes, Sir. May I make a suggestion?"

"Only if it will help the stealth approach."

"I suggest we enter the floor at 2:00AM after I make an alternate safety exit for you. I will scan for living things, then move back in time to a point where there is only one person on the level you want. That way, no one else will surprise you."

"Sounds good, little lady, but you don't know for sure if that person will be Professor Main, do you."

"No sir, but since you're disguised as a policeman, you could ask the person where he is."

"I'm not disguised. I *am* the police, and if your idea doesn't work I'll fry your circuits or something. But the strategy sounds OK. Let's do it."

The Bee plunged down in the darkness and landed just outside an exterior door. Connie reached out with her mechanical arm and broke the lock. "Would you like to walk in from here, or would you prefer to arrive in the professor's laboratory?"

"I want us inside. Make it a room right next to the lab."

The Bee entered the building as only a Bee can, and Connie began to scan. Gray shades of interiors flickered on the monitor screen, and finally they stopped. The exterior view screen displayed a small room with shelves. "We have time fixed at 7:30PM. This is a supply closet that adjoins the main laboratory."

"And why isn't it seven o'clock like I told you?"

"You gave me authority, sir. Two people were present in the lab until 7:20 PM. Remember, I opened the door leading to the basement stairway just in case you need to exit on foot. I can retrieve you on the outside if necessary."

"OK, OK, don't waste any more time. Open the hatch." Krajan awkwardly struggled out of the small opening while he jostled the mind probe device with one hand. Connie held out the tarpaulin. "Please cover the Bee with this for added security."

"Why don't you just do it yourself?"

"My arms are not long enough to throw it over the back. Sorry, Sir."

Krajan cursed, but complied. He poked his head back inside. "So, you're sure there's just one person on the other side of that door?"

"Yes, Sir. He is a male and working at the laboratory bench. He is the only one on this floor and there's no one on the three floors above. There are two people on the fourth floor who appear to be cleaning."

"Fine, fine, Computer Miss."

Krajan straightened his uniform, checked his concealed weapon for full charge, and slowly cracked the door ajar. He mumbled to himself: "Yeah, looks like Joseph Main, all right."

RECOVERY

Justin strode into the infirmary the next morning and found Anna sitting up on a bed and chatting with company. "Well, I'm glad to see we didn't lose our Comp Chief yesterday. You certainly look a lot better than last night, my dear. I see the swelling's down." He leaned in close to her. "And you're peeking out the other eye, too."

"Hi, boss. Great medical care plus lots of love and prayers here. The doctor explained his treatment, but I didn't understand a lot of it. He reset the broken bone under my eye, and the eye's going to be OK. I might be typing one handed for awhile, but hey, look at these two." She gestured at her guests. "I keep asking them leave, but here they are back again."

Singh and Sarah turned to grin at Justin. Sarah danced over and gave him a hug and a much appreciated kiss on the cheek. "Oh, Justy we *have* to stop those horrible people. They've always been awful, but they've never shot anyone in plain sight before."

Justy, now. He thought. “Not that you know of. But Sarah, you should assume this conversation is monitored, so we shouldn’t say any more.” He put his arm around her waist and turned toward Anna and Singh. “But I can tell you I just got back from a half hour with Margo. At first she feigned total ignorance of the incident, but then she claimed it ‘must have been justified’.”

Singh threw his hands in the air. “Nothing, absolutely nothing could justify that. Theft, criminal assault, and *murder*. Justify? And just so he could borrow a Bee?”

“Singh, my exact words with our esteemed Chairman. And there was a second murder too. Peter 640 was shot trying to get out a distress message. Well, Margo said she would ‘look into it’ and give me a report tomorrow. Anna, can you walk?”

Anna nodded her head and swung her legs off the side of the cot. This exposed the bright red locator glowing above her ankle. Sarah got her into a hospital robe, and slipped it over the half cast on her left arm. They filed out behind Justin’s ‘follow me’ motion, and walked down the hall to a small break room.

When the door closed, Justin motioned for Anna to sit down and he clamped a round metal device over her locator.

"We can talk in here. John took out the spy mikes for me this morning. This unit over Anna's leg is designed to pass on the locator beacon signal, but it blocks our voice transmissions. A little gift from Paul."

They gathered around a small table. "First, as I told John and Paul, I'm totally with you, and if you want my leadership, I'll do my best. Here's what I think we should do, but I'm open to your suggestions. The police have a heavy presence in both of our departure rooms, but nowhere else in the QDT right now. They won't station police everywhere until Krajan's scheduled return tomorrow tonight."

Singh leaned in and whispered. "How about we bring in fifty people of our own tomorrow, blast in, and just beat Krajan to death?"

Justin laughed. "A happy fantasy, but reality would leave us with fifty dead idealists and ten laughing police. No, we have to come up with something safer. Anna, first tell me why didn't you use your special powers to stop them and save yourself?"

Sarah and Singh turned to Anna for her reply, their puzzled eyes wide. "Out of instinct, I staggered the first one who took a swipe at me, but you had ordered me not to use the powers, remember? They would have kept sending in more police and eventually overpowered me, and then everyone would know what I can do."

"But, the next blow could have killed you. You don't need my permission to save your life."

"Singh did the saving for me." She turned to smile at him. "After Krajan's first sucker punch from behind, nothing much in my brain was working real well anyway."

Justin opened his hands toward the others. "When Anna transferred her cortex into the Connie Program, she then found herself able to control computers and implants at a distance. She reads minds too. It's our little secret. Make it yours."

Singh patted her shoulder. "But Anna, that wouldn't be a real defense against ten angry men, would it?"

"Sure it is. They'd collapse into a big sleepy pile together." She looked at Justin. "By the way Boss, never refer to Connie as a program. She really hates that."

Justin smiled. "OK, guys, what we'd really like to know is if there's any chance at all that Connie might actually be able to defeat Krajan's plan to get Spero. Anna?"

"Honestly, I can't think of anything. She knows that if Krajan thinks he was lied to, I'm toast. But she thinks differently than I do now. I've thought about writing a novel once, but she actually did, and in one year of on board time she's been to more places and times than anyone alive. She's been in close quarters with two men, and problem-solved their difficulties on the fly." Anna looked around the table with a big grin. "Course those are all things I'd just *love* to do."

Sarah laughed. "But, I'll say this. If anyone can figure out a solution, you can, er she can."

Justin coughed. "All right, people, I can see only three possibilities. One, Krajan will return with Spero tomorrow. Game over. All we could do is stage a public protest so *maybe* they won't execute him. The next most likely thing is he might return feeling betrayed, angry and empty handed." He lowered his gaze to Anna. "Unfortunately he'd try to make good on his revenge promise to kill you, my dear."

Singh said, "Well, we can be ready to remove Anna's locator. She can turn off her implant beacon on her own, and we know places where she can disappear."

"Exactly, and I already discussed this with Paul this morning. He's working on a plan with Gretchen for Anna's protection and hiding."

"Thanks everyone." Anna scratched her neck. "But you know he might just go after all of *you* instead. What's the third idea, Boss."

"This occurred to me later. It's also possible that Krajan could come back alone, with the information from professor Main and not feeling betrayed or angry. This would be because he just needed to work on the location data, or get new supplies or whatever. He'd be planning to go back and get Spero on a return trip."

Sarah reached for Justin's arm. "But that would just be postponing the first two possibilities, right?"

"Maybe not. Anna should be safe then, but Spero would still be in danger. Here's my idea. They'd need us to pull the ship's log and prepare the Bee for the next trip. We already have an emergency 'return to ship' beacon set on implant reception frequency…"

"Oh I see," Anna broke in. "We could send a secret message to Spero every time the Bee landed. I could do the modification myself so it would only be on Spero's ID frequency."

"Now does everyone see why I keep this smart little woman working here?" Justin chuckled. "At least we'd give Spero an alert, and a chance to hide. Meanwhile, I want everyone to go back to work as usual. They'll have the launch room cleaned up by noon."

Anna grabbed Justin's arm. "Boss, I'm sorry, I mean *Justin.* There's one more detail to take care of. Before they clobbered me, I had downloaded a duplicate of Connie. No one knows about it, but she's in a metal briefcase lying on the floor of my lab station. Remember Connie really *does* have all the data Krajan wants. Someone will have to be clever about securing it because they've probably restored complete video surveillance by now."

Sing leaned over and kissed Anna on the forehead. "That'll be my job, Anna." He grinned. "I wouldn't want to lose either one of you."

GOTCHA

Krajan slowly eased the door open, his portable memory scanner under his left arm, and a charged pistol in his right hand. He glanced right and left. No one else was in the laboratory except the Professor who was facing away, typing on a laptop. Joe didn't notice anything until Krajan placed his scanner on the lab table. Startled he swung around. "Ho! Who are you?"

Joe's eyes fixed at the gun pointed at him, and he slowly raised his hands. "I'm unarmed mister. Are you police, or did you come to steal? I don't have much on me. Wallet's in my right pocket. All yours."

"Shut up! Keep your hands up. Be nice and maybe you're not getting shot. Just need some info outa you."

"Sha--sure. Just put the gun down first. What do you want to know?"

A cynical thin-lipped smile spread across Krajan's face. "This could be very easy for you professor, or it could be very painful. Your choice. You should understand that I do know all about your wife, and your children, both homes too. Just give me the exact time and location where you left Spero 235, and they'll be fine."

Joe stood up in front of his lab stool and slid his hands onto its short metal back. *He won't shoot me until he knows.* "So, you're from 2247."

The intruder's eyes narrowed. "What a *professorial* deduction. Stop moving. We'll just do a little mind probe and it'll be all over."

"That thing makes me sick."

"I've got the juice that counters the hangover." He waved his gun at Joe's hand. "You know, I could take off one finger at a time."

Better let him think I'm cooperating. "OK, you tell me something I want to know, and I'll tell you where Spero is."

Krajan chuckled. "We both know you'd lie. Have to hook you up."

Joe gave a little shoulder shrug. "All right, I understand. Just tell me when the first Bee was launched, and you can go ahead."

Krajan moved his head closer and studied Joe's innocent expression. "That's all? Everyone knows the first

Bee flew in 2028." He holstered his gun. "Now sit back down."

Joe slid his right foot to brace it against the lab bench for take off. His peripheral vision spotted the stairwell door ajar almost behind him. "Well here's what I remember--I remember he didn't want to be found." He threw the stool at Krajan and sprinted for the escape. With a great roar Krajan tossed the stool aside and with two great strides caught him just as he reached for the door. He smashed Joe against the wall, and grabbed his neck with one huge hand. He dragged his weakly struggling prey to another stool and handcuffed him to it. "In my younger days, I'd of made it," Joe rasped.

"Well, aren't I lucky you're just weak and sickly now. Thanks for running, though. That was fun." Krajan backhanded Joe in the face resulting in blood oozing from one nostril.

Krajan pulled out needle electrodes from the probe machine and began sticking them into Joe's scalp. He sprayed a drug up his nose. "OK, now you're going back to a happy time in your past, you know, running all over time and places with your old buddy, Spero. Good times, right? Let's see where he wound up, huh Joe?"

Joe sat semi-conscious in the stool, flailing and twitching while Krajan wrote notes down from the little screen on the probe. Finally, he jerked out the wires. The left temple site bled freely from Joe's limp head running down his cheek to join the dried nose blood.

Krajan took out a second spray bottle and gave Joe a shot of it in the face. As Joe lurched into consciousness, Krajan chuckled. "Good thing I didn't decide to catch you back in eighty six, 'cause you really didn't know back then, huh? But Spero left you little notes and recordings. How nice of him." Krajan laughed. "So now we have the little perp in Corinth Greece three years into the reign of Tiberius. He's in love and sailing boats. How sweet. Should be easy enough to retrieve him." He kicked Joe in the shin.

Joe winced and scowled. "Why don't you just leave him alone? What harm's he doing."

Krajan switched the handcuffs, and left Joe with one hand free from the stool, the other still attached to it. "Yeah well, I would've preferred visiting Caligula or Nero. They knew how to have a real good time, but Tiberius did pretty well for himself in Capri. See, I slept with learning recordings."

Krajan picked up his uniform cap from the floor, and replaced it on his head. "Well, I tell you what. Since you were so 'cooperative' in…" Krajan laughed again. "in telling me just what I need to know, I'll tell you that Spero might actually live, only *might* is all I can say. I'll drag him before Aten, all right. But since Spero just went on a long vacation and didn't go to Egypt like we thought, maybe he'll get a slave's mercy, and just get tortured real good."

"You got the Bee back. Why go to all this trouble?"

Krajan beamed with the pride of his anticipated conquest. "Spero will just get what he deserves. I couldn't care less. But I'll get to the Supreme Directorate for sure. And when I hand over Spero in chains, I'll get a position in the Elect, complete with Aten's promise of eternal life. For this I think they'll even award me the Medal of Horus."

Krajan lightly swatted Joe in the ribs. "But at least I *know* I can count on a handful of virgins." He chuckled.

CONFRONTATION

Blessed are those who are persecuted
Because of righteousness,
For theirs is the kingdom of heaven. Mt 5: 10

John brought his scanning device and gave the QDT basement lounge a few turns to make sure no new electronic surprises had been added. Justin pulled out the air vent screen himself, checked for fiber optics, and replaced it. He had called an urgent meeting with Paul, John, Singh, and Sarah. Susan had also managed to slip away from her work.

Justin motioned for everyone to sit. "Paul brought me some sad reports an hour ago. This certainly won't appear in our media, but we all need to hear about it." He gestured for him to speak.

Paul leaned forward, cleared his throat and spoke in a low voice. "As you know, my job in our secret world is information and communications. None of you needs to be told that our beloved Aten is acting even more strangely than usual lately. He's doing some really cruel things and right out in the open."

Susan, the physician, nodded her head. "Possibly a psychotic break precipitated by his recent failures."

Paul went on: "We have a world network of people like me who share information when we can slip it through the jamming. Wish we had a better communications net, and we're working on improving it. Well, an hour ago there were simultaneous police raids on God meetings in almost every city. *Two* of them were in Jeru Dome. In that city police told local news they were looking for two terrorists and there were several casualties."

Sarah looked up. "Someone was hurt?"

"I'm sorry to say the police shot three people in Jeru Dome. The rest were dragged out and beaten. When an angry mass of their friends ran to help, a dozen were dropped by some kind of pulse weapon and hauled away. We've never seen this weapon, and our source didn't know if they died, but Aten's always been harder on this Dome for some reason."

John asked, “But what about the other cities? I heard someone was shot right here in Carolina. There are protesters outside the police headquarters right now.”

Paul nodded his head. “That’s right, and in other city raids there were five more shootings as well. What’s different in cities like ours is that there are no beatings in public, but everyone captured by the police are whisked off to parts unknown. Don’t look for any reports on this in our news.”

Sarah raised her hand and asked everyone to wait a moment. She bent down, turned her palms upward, and began nodding slightly. “Dearest merciful Lord, please forgive these men who were forced to commit evil crimes. Comfort the afflicted, we pray, and their families as only you can. We pray to...”

Susan handed her a tissue for her eyes. “We pray to you, oh God. May the strength of your faithful children inspire all of us in this testament to your glory.”

Susan, Paul and John said “Amen.”

Paul continued. “Fortunately, the other city meetings were dissipated with only minor injuries, but we lost the priest who presided at our Nile street meeting. We believe that surviving God Group leaders are flown to the psychiatric center at the SD. Most participants were sent to what they call retraining centers."

John raised an eyebrow. "Most?"

"Well, South Africa, at the shore colony down there…" Paul allowed a faint smile. "That's your old home, isn't it Sarah?"

"Yes, I've been to that marina as a little girl, It's beautiful. My mother might have been at a God meeting there. Is everyone all right?"

"Oh, fine, but they were meeting on a boat in the harbor when they were ordered to stop at gunpoint. A number of the townspeople had gathered to watch. The boat captain refused to come in so the police shot out its prow and sank it."

"Doesn't sound real fine, Paul."

Paul waved her off. "Well, they were all good swimmers and made it to the dock. This drenched assembly began to sing joyful hymns and wave their arms to a large crowd. Lots of people began to mingle and sing with them. The police could only watch while half the town sang praise songs. They surrounded and protected the group as they walked back home."

Sarah grinned. “Sounds like something my Mom and Dad would do.”

Susan sighed. “Well, that’s heartwarming, but it doesn’t change the awful pall of hopelessness in our cities right now. The Humwa and their sympathizers, namely us, do not have a world wide organization. We can’t even telephone other cities. Only Directors can.” She turned to Justin, and patted his shoulder. “So, like it or not Justin, you’re the closest thing we have to leadership right now. I think every Dome is hoping for some direction at this point, so what do you think we should do?”

Justin felt his pulse quicken in the warmth of those who turned toward him. He slid back in his chair and took a deep breath. “Well, first no one has officially made me a leader of anything, but I’ll give you my opinion. Aten’s crazy control freakishness is not going to go away, but he seems reluctant to provoke a large scale revolt.”

John said, “If he keeps pushing this way, he’ll get one though. Won’t he?”

Susan stood up and started pacing. “And this Psych Center at the SD really worries me. It’s the only one in the world. I’m the World Health Director and I’m not even allowed to go there, much less get follow-up reports on our people."

Justin said, "See, that's just part of his control thing."

"I hope that's all, but you should also know that I've never heard of anyone being discharged from that center."

Justin squinted at Paul. "Didn't you tell me you have an information contact at the SD? The Psych Building looked beautiful in the brochure. Try and find out about what actually happens to the patients there, OK?"

He motioned for Susan to sit back down. "OK, here's what I think we should do. First, every Dome will send a formal protest to their Chairmen and their SD representative. He'll be charged to demand a response from the SD. Second, have every city hold a peaceful, one hour demonstration protesting these raids. We'll be in front of Police Buildings in every city, just like a small group is doing right now."

John coughed. "You know if they're peaceful, they'll just ignore them."

"Perhaps, but I want the SD to see that we will escalate based on how they respond. As far as we know, their only means of counter-enforcement is a few tough cops, but I doubt they'll risk provoking everyone with more shootings."

John chuckled. "You might be right but we have no confirmation on that "sleep weapon" of theirs. Anyway, we'll pass the word. I'll just leave the diplomacy to you."

Justin grinned. "Thanks. Now speaking of diplomacy, Paul and I are on our way to see if we can get our building back and resume operations. I hate to say it, but once Spero is in custody everything should quiet down."

# # #

A few minutes later Justin and Paul stood in front of a hulking policeman barring the door to the secondary launch area. He scowled down at them.

"We have three Drones scheduled to launch this morning, officer. What harm could it do to let us carry on with our work?"

"All QDT launch sites are sealed until after the seventy-seven returns."

Justin tried to make eye contact with the officer. "Would you care to explain this directive? I see the Media have full access. They're everywhere today." He stood on tip toe and craned his neck. "That Bee will return to the main bay. What possible reason is there for us to be on lockdown on this one?"

"Police Director's orders."

"So you were instructed to explain nothing to us."

"You are a Director. You should call him."

Justin and Paul exchanged wry smiles. "The PD is not taking my calls, and the Chairman claims she knows nothing about what's going on. OK, tell me this. My employee, Anna 797, is feeling better now. May she go home?"

"Negative. She is confined to this building. House arrest."

Paul said, "And the charges? On what charges are you holding her?"

"Obstruction of justice…" He looked at Justin and his face relaxed. "Well I shouldn't tell you this, but I heard that if she's fully cooperative, the charge might be dropped when Krajan returns. She's needed in the development program for the eighty series, isn't she? The four-placer's an administrative priority."

The officer settled against the door frame. "Here's a suggestion, Director. Why don't you talk to her about not being a hostile witness? Krajan is due back in a few hours and he'll make a determination about the woman. Oh, by the way, if you need prison rations brought to her let us know."

Justin's shoulders slumped and he exhaled slowly. "You're too kind, Officer. No, we'll keep her fed, thank you." They turned to walk away and Paul put his hand on Justin's shoulder. "Did you see this morning's vid? Aten has scheduled an announcement for tomorrow afternoon. He probably expects it to be a victory proclamation for retrieving Spero today." "Yeah Paul, and a warning. Most likely he wants to hang Spero in front of the world the old fashioned way."

ARREST

Those who draw the sword

Will die by the sword. Mt: 26, 52

Krajan stood in front of Joe whose head was still floppy from the drugs. He started to remove the handcuffs, then pulled back and grinned. “Know what? I think I’ll just leave one cuff on for your own good. Wouldn’t want you to hurt yourself trying to be heroic.”

Joe’s tormentor picked up the memory scanner and his vid recorder. “It’s been fun, professor. It really has, but it’s time to load up and visit to your old buddy in Greece. I’m told those Roman Centurions knew how to have fun. Think I’ll find out in person.”

Krajan pulled open the door to the supply room with his foot. The room was filled with a large object under a green tarp. “Open up, Connie. Pull the cover inside.” Silence. He pulled a remote from his sleeve and clicked.

"Come on Connie. My hands are full. Open!" He swung around and snarled at Joe. "You *did* something, didn't you."

Joe shrugged his shoulders and shook his head. Krajan came out of the room still holding his devices, and the supply door closed behind him. He put them down on the lab table and his eyes narrowed as he approached Joe. He grabbed his neck. "You have an override remote from when you last flew it, don't you?"

Suddenly Krajan was startled to realize they were no longer alone. People had quietly slipped into the room when he was in the closet, and had spread out behind the lab bench. Expertly he swung behind Joe, drew him close for cover and pulled his weapon. He faced five policemen, guns in hand. "Glad you're here, officers. I've just arrested this man. You can take him in yourselves if you want." He pointed his stunner at Joe and stood him up by the back of his collar. "Here. He's all yours. You take the credit."

The police had formed a wide semicircle and held their revolvers pointed at Krajan. The one with the most hatch marks on his sleeve said, "And what are the charges, officer?"

Krajan casually took a step back toward the stockroom door and took Joe with him. "Drugs--I got him on drug possession. There on the table. Have a look at those bottles."

"Right, just a routine check, officer. You're not from our unit. May we see your badge?"

"Sure." Krajan flipped open the badge wallet and slid it across the table. "Ohio State Police, unit twelve."

The officer glanced at the badge. A flicker of a smile appeared and faded on his face. "All right, mister, please lower that gun thing and no one gets hurt."

"Yours first."

The officer in charge nodded to the others and they slowly placed their revolvers on the lab table in front of them. "Now yours. Then we'll take your prisoner just like you said."

They winced as Krajan quickly swept his stunner around. It made a clacking sound. He quickly repeated the process with the pistol from his uniform holster. It made a clinking sound. He threw them both away with a curse.

Joe saw the knife coming out and instinctively spun off the stool and held it as a shield between them. The officers ran around the table and quickly piled on the writhing, swearing Krajan. It took four of them to disarm, cuff and shackle him while the fifth struggled to remove his weapon belt. This last policeman wound up sitting on the floor against the wall next to Joe. Both were breathing hard.

When the officers pulled Krajan upright, he began raging. "You just don't understand. I'm from the future police, and this man's in my custody. Look in that room if you don't believe me. My ship's in there."

One officer opened the supply door, and held it open for the others to see. He turned back smiling. A green tarpaulin lay crumpled on the floor of the empty room. "No, no. It was *there*. He must have the remote. That's it. Now I *know* he does. Search him!" Four men began to drag the struggling, cursing Krajan toward the exit.

The fifth officer released Joe from the chair. "Well, at least it seems his toy key unlocks your cuffs." They still sat on the floor together. "Are you OK Professor? Looks like you've been bleeding. I can call a paramedic."

"I'm OK, really. Just one bump on my face. How'd that guy get in here, anyway?"

"He broke the side door lock. What a nut case, huh?" Krajan could still be heard screaming in the distance as he was dragged down the hall, but now he had begun to swear in TL. "Look, just rest up, professor. We'll send someone by tomorrow to take a statement. Sorry about this."

The officer helped Joe up. He proceeded to put on a rubber glove, gather up Krajan's weapons and drop them into plastic bags.

Joe said, "Do you have to take those?"

"Yeah. Evidence. The ray gun looks like a toy, though." Gesturing toward the lab table he said "Those chemicals and all that electronic stuff yours?"

"Yes."

"OK, professor, we'll make a complete search of the building before we lock up. I'd say he's a loner but we'll check anyway. Here's my card and cell number. Just call if you need anything."

Joe shook his hand and smiled. "I'll be fine, really. Can't thank you enough. You guys are lifesavers."

"Glad to help, sir." Big smile. "See you tomorrow."

Joe sat at his lab bench for awhile. He rubbed his sore head, blotted the dried blood off his cheek, and carefully folded up the wires on the memory probe. The thumping, slamming sounds of the police checking the building died down, and Joe swiveled on his stool to survey the damage to his lab. A whoosh and a flash from behind made him jump up. *It's in the supply room.*

Joe picked up a Bunsen Stand for protection just in case, and slowly opened the door. *Ah ha,* he thought. He was confronted a yellow, crackling sphere. *The Bee's back, but maybe there's another agent inside.* He raised his 'weapon' as the hatch slid up. No one got out. "Anybody home?"

"Hi, Joe. Just me. Come on in for a minute."

Joe peeked inside. "Connie, that's really you isn't it? You're alive! I'm so glad."

"Of course it's me. I heard what happened on the police radio. Have a seat so I can have a look at you." Joe awkwardly clambered into the Bee and sat in the old familiar soft gray chair. "There you are. Twenty three years older, and just as handsome."

"And there you are, just as flirtatious as ever."

Connie laughed. "Joe first, I gotta know. Our records only show you married, no name of spouse. Is it Melissa?"

"Course it is, Miss Matchmaker."

"Ah Ha! He, he, he. And you have kids?"

"Lucy, almost twenty one, and Matt seventeen. We call him Newt."

"Ahaaaa. That's so great, and I *so* want to meet all of them."

"Sure, but first how 'bout telling me what the heck *this* was all about. I know he was after my information on Spero, and I think he got it too. But why did he come dressed as a train porter with useless weapons?"

"OK, well for us it's just a few months later in 2247, and we thought they had given up on Spero, but some crazy group of top cops didn't. So you met Krajan, right?"

"A gorilla with the charm of a rattlesnake. Want his equipment back?"

"Oh, yes. Don't want to leave future tech behind, and I have to erase your mind probe data from his recorder."

"But, they have his stunners."

"Not really. Those are just plastic look-alikes with metal weights inside, the pistol too. While he was in stasis I made fakes of everything, including his gravity locator, but I have to chuckle at my best idea. I added a tiny "Made in China" on each of them."

Joe laughed. "No, no, I thought your *best* was the 'Junior Detective' badge and the uniform." He laughed again. "A *train porter's* outfit, and one from the Nickel Plate Railroad, even. That line's extinct, you know, but if I hadn't thought the guns were real, I'd of put up a better fight. Seriously though, this guy really did find out where Spero lives, so what's next?"

"Well, here's the lucky part, Joe. Krajan had downloaded all the police records from your time in Ohio. When he was in stasis, I gave him the identity of a 2002 murderer captured in 2009. They had no DNA, but did have fingerprints. While he was in stasis I changed Krajan's prints to match his."

"Wow, Connie—you can do that? Say, they might execute him."

"They will. Records show the execution in 2010. They also catch the other guy, but that's in 2012."

"But, isn't that a bit…"

"Harsh? That devil shot an innocent, unarmed woman just before he got on board, someone I knew, too. If his unit rescues him they'll go and kill Spero. And he's killed many others before that. Besides, he beat up Anna real bad. He threatened to kill her too if I didn't cooperate, and he meant it. Pretending to play along kept her alive for the time being."

Joe sat back in the seat and thought a moment. "I see you're point. I'm not for Capital Punishment, but I understand. Justice done. But, how'd you get the cops to come?"

"Oh, just a hysterical 911 call from a girl who saw the break in and reported violence on the fourth floor. I used a cell phone number that was reported stolen earlier this afternoon."

"Connie, you really are brilliant, and a lot of people are really grateful--especially me."

"You're welcome, but now we have to figure out what to do next."

"Oh, right. I remember. You can't go home all by yourself, so now you'll want me to face the firing squad again."

Connie giggled. "No, no. I wouldn't do that to you again. Let's think about it for awhile. You take your car back home." She handed him a locator. "This one's real. I'll meet you and the family in three hours, OK?"

MELISSA

While Joe slid all the furniture to the side of their living room, Melissa poured coffee into a Thermos beside a plate of cookies. "I'm just sad Lucy isn't here to see this, Joe. It would mean a lot to her."

"Oh, she'll still get to see a Bee. Heck, in the future she's the one who actually *builds* the first one. And by the way, Connie isn't going to be eating those cookies, dear. We will."

"I know, I know. I'm just excited. I've never seen one of these crazy Bees you always talk about." She peeked under the Band Aid on Joe's temple, and patted it down. "Is this ship thing really going to come down right through our roof?"

"Yup, sort of. Won't hurt anything though." Having cleared a landing spot, Joe placed the little disc in the center of the living room. He stood against the wall, put his arm around his wife, and checked his watch. "Should be here any second now. Remember what I said to expect. I promise it's harmless."

In the next room their cat hissed and scrambled down the hall hotly pursued by Calliente's clicking nails on the hardwood. Melissa turned to the doorway. "Stop it you guys or I'll…" Suddenly a whoosh of warm air and a bright yellow-green sphere filled the center of the room.

"She's right on time," Joe said, trying to release Melissa's "claws" from his body. The ship's feet slowly came out and the crackling craft gently settled down on the rug. When the hatch opened, Joe pranced over and poked his head inside. "Sorry the kids aren't here Connie, but Melissa's anxious to see you."

Joe climbed in but popped his head out a moment later to check Melissa. She was flattened against the wall. "Oh come *on*, dear. You're not going to trust me alone in here with this romance novelist, are you?"

Melissa ambled over toward the Bee trying to appear casual. She glanced up to inspect her ceiling for damage. "Smells like ozone." She knelt down in front of the hatch, gingerly touched the metal opening but pulled back quickly. "It's cold."

Joes arms extended out to help her in. "Yes, but it's warm inside. Just pretend its Newt's old tree house."

Melissa reached in with a trembling hand. Joe pulled her up. "Remember, I've been telling everyone you're fearless."

That made her laugh. "Of the jungle, maybe. This is really quite something else."

They settled into their seats, and Melissa swiveled her head around to take in the strange interior. "Connie, you're real quiet. Did you know Melissa made you some cookies?" This got him a quick swat.

Finally two of Connie's arms came out of the nacelles and their hands clasped in front of them. "I've just been admiring you two. Oh, you guys are really too cute and didn't I just *know* you'd be together?"

"Well, thanks for knocking some sense into him, Connie. It's really great to finally meet you. Lucy got your book published, and it's doing well, too. I hope you don't mind that it was edited and she's raking in the profits. I have a CD copy for you."

"Wow, that's exciting. Glad she's getting paid for her effort. Say, Joe--we have some serious girl talk to do. Do you mind for a few minutes?"

Joe chuckled and clambered out. "Oh, I get it. Just don't burn me too badly. I'll be in my study."

For over an hour Joe could hear them in the next room chatting and laughing, but when he realized Melissa had moved to the bedroom he went in after her. "So what's up?"

Melissa was laying out clothes on the bed. "Oh, Hi. We have it all figured out. You don't have to take her back. Could be dangerous if you went. No telling if they'd still be angry about your escape."

"I see where you're going with this. Wait, maybe it's just as dangerous for you."

"Nah, Connie found something in her 'history' records. I give a speech at the Anthropology Society convention eight months from now. Interesting. They haven't called to invite me yet."

Joe nodded. "And, of course, I can't come with you 'cause this Bee only seats two and a future someone has to bring you back."

Melissa gathered up the clothes she selected and tucked them under one arm. "Exactly, but Connie expects to have me back the day after tomorrow on your time. There's some left over lasagna in the fridge."

Joe grinned and shook his head. He stood in front of his wife and held her arms. “Why do I have the sudden feeling that you’re really enjoying this whole idea? She promised you a place to visit, didn’t she?”

Melissa’s gray-blue eyes sparkled and her body gave a quick wiggle. “Uh huh.” She kissed him quickly and picked up her travel bag. “I’d like to say I’ll call you when I get there, but you know how that is.”

He gave her a squeezy kiss. “Well, anyway, I get all the cookies. Just you be careful, darling. Via con Dios.”

# # #

“And so that’s the basics of Bee travel, Melissa. Now I know I promised you one stop along the way, but you’re going to be all alone when you go outside. That’s why we have the rule that requires two people for field excursions, excepting rescue and retrieval of course.”

“Well then, could you guarantee that the person who’d return with me would allow me a side excursion?”

“Nope. They almost certainly wouldn’t.”

“There, you see Connie, this is my only chance.”

“But wouldn’t it be almost as good if we did fly-overs? You could take all the pictures you want.”

“Uh, uh. You promised, remember? California coast, twenty thousand BC or bust. Should be about glacial maximum.”

Connie threw up her metal arms. “OK, OK, but you’re my responsibility and, I’m not even sure how to dress you.”

“Brought my own. Let’s make the arrival in July. Connie, I’m not trying to blend in. I just want to make contact. Primitive people aren’t likely to attack one person just because they wear funny clothes. In fact that’ll make them curious.”

“But if I have to, I can charge at them with the Bee and scare them off.”

“Yes, and Connie, I do have your stunner thing, so don’t worry. I’ll be fine.”

“Melissa.”

“Yes?”

“You’re going to be the first real live woman to ever fly in a Bee.”

ALONG THE WAY

"All right, Melissa, we're hovering over the coordinates you gave me: we're at five kilometers altitude, and it's twenty thousand years BC, western coast of North America."

"The exact spot where my cave is?"

"Well, close. I had to adjust for the crustal movements of dozens of earthquakes that will come later. Your cave's moved about thirty meters southeast."

Melissa scrunched down by the transparent hatch. "Oh, Connie, it's just beautiful, isn't it. Look at those blazing white snowy peaks. The coastal land's lush and green, but just a little streak along the shore. It's all snow and ice to the east."

"We're not quite dead center on glacial maximum. There's a narrow patch of water west of the land that will be Alaska, but you could swim across if it weren't so cold. But by the way, it's sixty eight Fahrenheit down on the beach."

"Can we fly any lower without being seen?"

"Sure, Dear, but I already scanned the shore while you were getting dressed. There's a small boat with two people in it a half click north, and there are three people walking along the shore down toward the spot you picked."

Melissa plopped back in her seat and started checking items in her khaki side bag. She wore camouflage print Bermuda length shorts, a tan shirt, and a big smile. "Great. Let's park this thing away from the beach a ways and out of sight so it doesn't frighten them. I think it's best if the people walk along and just find me."

Connie chuckled. "I'll see if they have a parking lot behind that outcropping." She handed her a gun. "Put this in your bag. I took out the chip so anyone can fire it. It's only set to disable people, so you won't hurt anyone, I promise."

"Really, I don't think…"

"Melissa, I have to insist. I'll never forgive myself if something happens to you. Remember, we can't stay long. I can see and hear everything from the camera I put in your hair to record this, so you don't have to shout if you need me, OK?"

Connie picked out a crevasse along the cliff face. She snuggled the Bee into it and the tarp completed the cover up. A rocky outcropping extended out toward the water so

Melissa would be hidden from the beachcombers until they rounded it.

She walked out to a driftwood log, sat down and waited. "Connie, can you hear me OK when I speak quietly like this?"

"Loud and clear, my dear."

"OK, record everything. I think I'll just narrate this as it happens." She looked all around her and up at the cliff face. "There's the sea caves. They're higher up now with the sea this low."

Melissa opened the pack between her legs and arranged things for easy access. "No one around yet, Connie. Just a beautiful sunny day in California. I should have brought a bathing suit and a beach chair."

Melissa sat patiently. All she could hear was the repeating rush of the waves, but her peripheral vision was attuned to the rocks on the right. Finally, people came sauntering around. They stopped and stared at her for a few cautious moments, but she pretended not to notice, and began to dig with a stick.

"I glanced at them, Connie. Looks like a woman with two children."

A young girl broke away and ran toward her despite a protesting maternal voice. She stood in front of Melissa bright eyed, and watched her dig. “Connie, she’s about five years old. Dressed in skins of some kind and I think that’s a dried kelp mesh she’s wearing as a wrap around. She’s tanned ‘cause she’s pale under her chin.”

The girl came closer and Melissa looked up and smiled. The girl smiled back and fearlessly took Melissa’s hand, leading her closer to the water. “She doesn’t look Asian or fully Caucasian either. Hair’s a tangled mess. She wants to show me something. Her mother’s coming over now, probably with her older brother.”

The girl let go of Melissa’s hand, pointed to some bubbles in the sand and looked up with a grin. She and her brother dug vigorously with curved flat sticks and she pulled up a clam. She washed it in the next wave and presented it to Melissa. “I’m smiling and nodding, Connie, can’t believe this. The kids just gave me a lesson in how to dig clams.”

Melissa took the clam, and signaled for them to wait while she went back for her bag. She plunked down on her knees in front of the girl when she returned, and gave her a big open mouthed smile. She reached in, pulled out a shell necklace, and placed it over the girl's head. The girl gave a happy laugh and Melissa got a sandy, wet hug.

The mother pulled her child back, but she was smiling too, and said something. "I'm guessing she said 'I tell her not to talk to strangers, but she just won't listen. Sorry.' Now the brother is kneeling in front of me. I think he wants a prize too."

Melissa held up her clam, smiled at the boy and tilted her head. Both mother and son went to work, avidly digging up the beach. The boy presented his clam first. When Melissa handed him a shark tooth arm band he let out a whoop followed by a few jumping dance steps.

The woman cautiously presented her clam. Melissa took out a large plastic comb and first demonstrated how to use it on her own hair. The mother allowed her to comb her hair, pull out the tangles, and snap in a hair clasp behind her neck. Her eyes grew wide with excitement. She felt her smooth chestnut hair sliding easily through her fingers, and began to giggle.

"OK, Connie, they're bowing and moving away. That went really well and I have lots of hair roots I can bring back for testing. I'm truly amazed at how relaxed and non-threatened they seem. The very fact that there are even *people* here just casually strolling around is completely amazing too. They've got to be pre-Clovis, probably the same people we found in Sandia Cave, New Mexico.

She began to close her bag and get up. "Uh oh. Here comes Papa."

A slender man wearing a loin skin gracefully pranced over with a fishing spear held over his head. He approached with stealthy measured steps, as though he were looking for the right moment to hurl his spear. He looked sternly at Melissa, then toward his family. He bellowed something loudly to them down the beach, and the mother shouted back. "Hopefully she put in a good word for me."

"Connie, get a look at this guy. What a hunk. I'm extending my arms out, palms up and smiling. He understands I'm friendly and unarmed. Course I'm lying about unarmed part."

The man backed away and waved for the others to keep on walking. "He seems basically uninterested in me. Darn. I feel so scorned. Guess he was just checking my threat potential. Notice the sack tied to his waist. He's got the catch of the day in there."

When the four had disappeared behind the rocks, Melissa ran back to the hidden Bee, and slid into the hatch.

"Omygod. That was so *great*, Connie. I shouldn't have given her my hair clasp, I know. That might survive and give some other archeologist a fit one day." She laughed. "Can we get a close up shot of their boat without scaring them?"

Connie was swaying her arms to music: "We'll have fun, fun, fun, 'til Daddy takes the T-bird away."

Melissa plunked into her seat and the music stopped. "OK, you know I'd just love to stay all day and go up to those caves. I can see smoke coming out of one of them."

"No, no. Please, Dear. We've broken enough rules for one day, and going into a cave by yourself--that's really risky." The hatch closed, and the Bee silently glided up the beach a hundred meters up. It hovered over the little boat while Melissa took photos before they swooped away from the Earth. "What are you going to do with that hair and those shell things?"

Melissa sighed and pouted. She took out the hair clump and wrapped it in a plastic sandwich bag she had in her pouch. "Well, the hair roots will give us a DNA sample to compare with other populations and help pin down their ethnic origin." Melissa put her hand over her mouth and looked up at Connie's eye.

"What's the matter, Melissa? You look upset."

"It's her face, Connie. I just realized. She didn't look like Lucy, but her eyes had the same 'Oh look, Mommy, come let me show you' expression. The girl didn't care at all if I looked different from any woman she'd seen before. To her I was just a Mommy."

Melissa turned away and wiped an eye. Connie said "OK, now I see tears. Look dear, that girl and her family have great lives. Don't you start worrying about *her,* now."

"No, they don't. It's a really hard life. It might be summer now, but…"

The two were silent for awhile. "There's something else, isn't there Melissa?"

"I…I can't help thinking. When I looked into that child's face--was I seeing someone who would start a family with a hundred branches and a thousand children? Or…" Melissa quickly put her head down.

"Or?"

"Or--was she the little girl whose bones I found in that cave."

Connie began to gently massage her shoulders with metal fingers. "Oh, Melissa, I'm sure she wasn't. Your date could be hundreds of years off either way and besides, this girl looked really healthy. There's no point--you'll never know anyway, will you?"

Melissa sat up and gamely smiled into Connie's eye. "I know, I know. I shouldn't get emotional, but anthropology never got so *personal* before. I know I'll always remember her happy little face, but--I'll be fine, really. You're such a good friend, Connie. Thanks."

"All right now. The real question is what are you going to do with those stinky shells?"

"The clams? I was hoping I could trade them for something good when I meet the natives of 2247."

Laughter cascaded from Connie's speaker. Finally she said, "You know, you're probably right. Clams sure aren't on our menu back home. Give them to me. I'll keep them cool for you."

"Oh good, cause they'll definitely smell wretched if they sit around for twenty thousand years."

COMING HOME

"Melissa, are you awake? We'll be landing soon."

Melissa's body jerked into awareness, her eyes still clouded. "What, what…" Comprehending her strange surroundings took a moment, but she yawned, stretched and rumpled her hair. "I must look *dreadful*, Connie. That knockout thing gave me a hangover."

"Here, drink this. You didn't bring any toiletries?"

"Nah, I thought I'd use the free ones at the hotel."

Connie giggled. "OK, I'll show you how to wash up on board. I made you a ladies shirt and a pair of fitted slacks. Only kids wear shorts in my time."

Melissa held them up. "Nice tailoring. The salmon and lime combination looks pretty cool too. Thanks. So what's our plan?"

"Right now we're out of sight behind the moon. Unfortunately, our usual landing spot is an armed camp at the moment, so we're going to show up in friendlier territory."

"But you said all of your cities were under the same control."

"True, but we good guys have hiding places nearby."

"Right, but, won't they see us when we fly down?"

"Leave that to me. We'll avoid detection by fixing in time right over the South Pole. Next we'll blast into the ice and rock—we don't *blast* really—not to worry."

Connie twirled her fingers as though she were pointing to a globe. "From there we follow the Mid-Atlantic Ridge around South America and head for the Continental Shelf. After that we zip through the upper mantle and come up in a shielded tool shed half a kilometer west of Carolina Dome."

Melissa stared at Connie's eye with a slack jaw. Connie added, "Oh, and after that we get a return pilot for you and he'll do the same route in reverse."

"Sorry I asked. Mind if I keep my eyes closed? But say, as long as I'm going to suffer through this—I hope you won't hate me for another request. I'd like to see what happened to our mountain retreat in your time—wouldn't have to get out of the Bee or anything risky. I just want to have a quick look."

Connie quietly thought for a few moments. "Yeah, OK—I guess I'm kinda curious myself. That was the survival burrow Joe built, huh?"

"Right, and I might be disappointed if it's all destroyed, but I'd like to know."

"Most everything was destroyed Melissa, but there are people hiding out from Aten in small settlements. They're scattered all around the world. Give me a sec, I'll check our survey.—OK, tell you what. I can come up on the little hill across from the stream. We can check it out first with the scope."

# # #

When they broke the surface and stopped, Melissa cheered. "Connie, that was the scariest ride like *ever*. It was like the horror tunnel in an amusement park."

"Well, you asked for it, dear. Telescope's by the hatch. My scan didn't show any people outside."

Melissa settled in cross-legged behind the little transparent door. "Well, it's just good to see rocks and trees." She squinted into the eyepiece. "OK, that's our mountain all right—house is gone—kind of a mess--just some burnt timbers—let's see. Would it hurt to move in closer, maybe down by the stream?"

"Sure, looks like there's no one here."

"Oh, that's better. There are some posts where the deck used to be and whoa!"

"Whoa, what?"

"There's our entrance to the cavern. Our wooden doors are gone but there are new ones. Looks like steel doors painted the same color as the granite. I think there might be some people living inside."

"There sure are. Someone just scanned us."

Melissa chuckled. "So my burnt up house is camouflage for anyone who might be looking. I'm just glad someone's using the cavern. Oh look, there are corn and tomato plants growing along the old drive an…"

The hatch suddenly closed. "Sorry dear but they're not sociable. They just trained a laser guided weapon on us. Hang on. I'll have us in Carolina in ten minutes."

# # #

Melissa relished stepping into the sunshine. She took a deep breath, walked out of the wooden shack, and adjusted the earpiece Connie gave her. “I’m going to tell you again. That was another hugely scary ride, young lady. You hear me all right, Connie?”

“I hear you just fine, dear, but please don’t go wandering too far off, OK? If our arrival triggered the intruder alert in the shack, one of our good guys should come along soon.”

“I know, I know. I’ll sit and wait until someone comes for me. You’re sure this is our future? Looks more like an ancient farm to me.”

“It’s peaceful out here, isn’t it? We farm land that’s out of sight from the city. I think this was a corn crop they just harvested. Look over by that large tree to the North where the woods begin.”

“I see it, Connie.”

“One of my, or I mean Anna’s, friends made a flower garden in a forest clearing there. It has benches and a little bubbly brook. Someone called it the ‘meditation garden’ and it stuck. Lots of people go to sit there whenever they can sneak out of the Dome.”

“Just to look at flowers?”

“I know. Maybe that seems commonplace in your century, Melissa, but it’s a rare treat here. Some go there to paint, or to write, others just to relax and think. Others simply enjoy having a quiet place to meditate and pray."

"I thought you said religion was forbidden here."

"It is, unless you call worshiping our Supreme Director a religion. People meet in secret God meetings as they call them. Mostly Jewish and Christian, I think. Anna went to one called *Waters Alive* with Sarah once."

"Does Anna think there's a God? My Joe became a believer all on his own one day, just poof, out of the blue."

"Anna's still on the fence, but as for myself, I figured out that God is alive and well based on math and the improbability of this universe. I'll have to talk to her about that sometime."

Melissa laughed. "You just figured it out? I'd like to hear about *that*. But why wouldn't you both feel the same way? You and Anna have the same brain."

"I have more thinking time than she does. It's simple mathematics really. There are almost a thousand variable entities like the mass of a proton, its rate of decay, strength of gravity, strength of the forces that hold atomic nuclei together, and lots more too."

"So the universe is complicated. What's that prove?"

"Well, there are about a billion different *values* that each one of those could actually be set for, and changing any of them would lead to either *no* universe with stars, or very unstable systems. No life, at any rate."

Melissa sat down on a stump and searched the horizon. "So we're just lucky to be in one of the many universes that works, huh?"

"It's not luck. Even in our time there's no evidence that one single *second* universe exists. In order to get ours by chance--well it would be like winning a billion to one lottery a billion times in a row."

"Oh Connie, you sound like a Divinity student I had in my class. That doesn't prove there's a God."

"Maybe not, but it surely seems that some person tinkered with a lot of possible settings just to get a universe made specifically for life. Sherlock Holmes said: *When you eliminate the impossible, whatever remains, however improbable, is the truth."*

Melissa strained to see anything where the city dome was supposed to be, but all she could glimpse was an occasional glimmer through the hilltop trees. "OK, OK. I'm sure Joe would love your argument. We'll talk lat…"

"Melissa, could you come back in here, please? I need you."

She slipped back into the shack. The ozone from the glowing Bee tickled her nose and she sneezed. "Sure, what's up?"

"Seems we have a little problem. No one knows we're here. We've buried some wires that go from this shack to our little community outside the Dome, and a sensor in here should have alerted the science lab of our arrival. See that little yellow light in the corner? It will turn to green when someone returns the signal. Nothing so far, so probably there's no one's in the lab."

"Hmmm. And you can't fly there or use wireless, because the bad guys would find us. But why don't I just walk up there?"

"You might have to risk it, dear. But I want to try something first. There's a telephone on the wall below the light, something like the ones you're used to, but it only calls three places. I can't pull it inside with me, but if you punch in 003, it will signal the QDT basement lounge."

Melissa picked up the receiver. "Got it."

"Tell me who answers first. Say 'Che is yamma?'"

She leaned on the wall and stared back at the hatch opening with a scrunched up expression and waited for someone to answer. Finally, “Ya?”

“Hello, I mean Che is yamma?”

“Goreh deu sank zero”

Melissa held the phone and called the words back into the hatch for Connie. She replied. “He’s OK. Say ‘Deu mil Anglais, danka.’”

Melissa returned to the phone and listened. “Oh, good. So you’re Gary and speaking English now. Listen, I’m Melissa Main, the Professor’s wife. I just flew in with Connie in Bee 77. We’re down at your little shack.”

She covered the phone and called into the hatch. “He seems real happy.”

“OK, Gary. See you in a few minutes.”

Melissa chatted with Connie for awhile, and went back outside to wait. “Hold on Connie, I see some movement up there on top of the rise.”

A man came into view at the far edge of the cornfield wearing coveralls. He began to jog down one of the rows with a briefcase in one hand. “Here he comes, Connie.”

Gary 250 was very polite when he realized he was actually talking to Professor Main’s wife, and he was ecstatic to learn that Krajan was defeated. "I believe I'll be the one taking you home, Mrs. Main, but first there are several people who would like to talk with you. Hope you don't mind."

"Of course, but Connie's the real hero here."

Gary carried his metal "briefcase" to the Bee, pulled out a cable from it and put his head and shoulders into the hatch. His muffled voice replied, "OK, she'll get to tell her story too." He came out of the Bee, smiled at Melissa, and patted the case that now contained Connie. "Let's go."

NEW PLANS

Justin, Paul, John and Susan slipped away to the Science Lab when the news was whispered in their ears. They listened in slack-jawed silence to Connie and Melissa's account of how Krajan's plan had been foiled. Justin apologized to her for not allowing a tour of the Dome—too dangerous, but as a consolation, he sent her off with a guide to spend some time exploring Saunders.

Meanwhile, they gathered around a worktable in the Science Lab to review their choices. "Well, guys," Justin gushed. "This is one time when I couldn't be happier to be wrong. It's so unexpected, so--*wonderful*. Did it even occur to anyone here that Krajan wouldn't be coming back? How do you think we should play this, John?"

John put his hand on Gary's shoulder and gave it a little shake. "The less they know the better. I hate lying, but for everyone's protection, we need a good story. When Gary told me about Bee 77's return, I asked him if he would take her back. He's one of us but he happened to be in your break-room at the time. Gary's on my outside crew clearing tree branches near the Dome. He's brave, and he's single too—no family."

John looked at Gary who returned an "aw, gee" look. "However, it seems he's lazy." Gary returned a "what, me?" look.

"Yes, lazy. What were you doing in that lounge on a workday, Gary?"

"I—I was on break. Rachel invited me."

John laughed. "OK, he could say Melissa took him at gunpoint. What does everyone think?"

Susan stood up. "No, keep Melissa out of this, but we need a credible story. We don't want these crazy guys going back for revenge. If Krajan is to be executed for murder anyway, why not say that a twenty first century policeman brought the Bee back, and they have him on murder charges for killing a policeman."

Justin bounced his fist on the table. "Yes, and that's almost correct, too. It's reasonable that they would have sent the Bee back in a courtesy from one force to another."

Susan: "What?"

"A courtesy. We have a protocol for that. The twenty first century man would get in the Bee and our emergency recall program would explain it to him. Who would turn down an adventure like this? Our story will be that the policeman requested a landing outside, and Gary was the first person he found. He'd be working on the trees, right?"

"And, *and…*" Paul broke in, "He could deliver Krajan's indictment for murder and request non-interference."

Susan dropped her head. "Remember, he really *did* murder poor Trish."

Melissa had carried a bag from the Bee. John picked it up from the table. "What's this?"

"Krajan's guns, his real ones." Connie's muffled voice came out from the case. "Why'd you close me up again? It's stuffy in here."

Justin chuckled and snapped open the briefcase. "Sorry, Connie. We were ignoring you, weren't we?"

"Hmphh. You'd think I was invisible or something. Anyway, I put his chips back in the guns and his prints are intact. Joe only picked them up by the barrel."

"Hey, that's great," John said. "We'll make sure they've been fired and remove any trace of the Professor."

Justin turned to Paul, his eyes squinted. "Can you make up a credible document for Gary when he returns?"

Paul shrugged. "I could try if I…"

Connie interrupted, "I printed some blanks from the Ohio Police archives."

Paul waved his hand. "But wait. There's still one more thing. We'll have to connect Gary to the memory probe when he's back in orbit and erase his memory of Melissa. Can you handle that, Connie?"

"As Joe used to say: 'piece of cake'. I'll add an image of a twenty first century policeman staring at him."

Justin nodded at the smiling faces around the table. "OK, that's the plan. Not only will the plotters know they were defeated again, but this time they did the unpardonable act of messing with the past and exposing our present day problems. We'll make sure the world knows."

Susan said, "Lets hope they will leave us alone after this. You know, most of our regular police have never been a part of…" She jumped up and signaled everyone to be quiet. "Shhhh, do you hear that?"

Justin whispered back. "The troops are coming?"

Susan grinned. “No, it’s music. Listen.” She hastened to the door and opened it so everyone could hear. “Come on.” She beckoned. “It’s coming from the repair shop.”

They quietly hastened to the repair shop and stood against the wall in awe. Incredible sounds filled the room. Melissa was playing a cello, her eyes closed in concentration. Finally she finished and looked up, startled by the audience. “Oops, sorry. I didn’t see you come in. I hope it’s all right. This just relaxes me.”

Susan was the first to speak. “My God, Melissa. That was so, so—absolutely wonderful.” They all applauded. “What was it?”

“Oh, thank you. I don’t have the last measure quite right yet. It’s ‘Jesu, Joy of Man’s Desiring’, by Bach. First piece was Vivaldi’s Largo.” She motioned to her guide sitting in the corner. “He’s been recording it.”

Justin said “I hope you’ll let us record some more music before we send you back.” Gary appeared in the doorway. “But if she’s ready to go I guess that had better be soon.”

Melissa grinned widely. “Okay, I hate to leave you nice people, but here’s a little song that’s appropriate for the occasion.”

She began to play and sing along: “It was *grea*t fun, but it was just one of those things--just one of those *crazy* things--just one of those *bells* that now and then rings--it was *great* fun, but it was just one of those things.” She bowed to laughter and applause. “That, my friends, was Cole Porter.” John gingerly took the cello in both hands and leaned it gently against the work bench. “The craftsman who restored this just finished last week. Wish he could have been here to hear it being played.”

“Whose cello is it, John? The bridge is set kinda high. Makes playing it harder, but it has beautiful tone.”

John glanced around. “I’ll tell him about the bridge. Well I guess this instrument really belongs to all of us.”

Susan gave Melissa a hug and locked her gaze. “Melissa, Dear, this cello is the only one that exists in the whole world.”

SURPRISE VISIT

"Uh, Chief Sir, thank you again for letting us cover this event live and worldwide. The camera behind me will show you sitting in the control room, but with a split screen, we'll show the Bee arriving with the other one."

The Police Chief didn't look up from the view screen in front of him. "May I send my camera man into that inner room and shoot the scene when the Bee appears out of nowhere?"

The Chief leaned into the screen, put a thick index finger on a number, and tapped the keyboard. "Sure, walk right into the Clean Room if you want, but hold your breath since all the air's been pumped out." He chuckled.

The announcer squirmed in silence for awhile. The Chief half turned to him with an expression of impatient condescension. "Should be another view port around that corner, but you can't use this one next to me." He dismissed him with a wave of his hand. “No more questions. I’m busy.”

The reporter and his camera men quietly backed up along the circular path that surrounded the Clean Room. He found a QDT technician who looked up, and he stuck out his microphone. Just above a whisper, he asked: “Most of our viewers have never seen a manned Bee coming in on a live broadcast. Our history video only shows a Drone. Sir, how do we know the ship will arrive at this exact time?”

A boyish looking man swiveled around in his terminal and grinned. “Because the return time was inputted before the departure.”

The reporter beckoned for the camera to show a close up of the Tec. “Well, please tell us more. What if the officer took longer than he expected?”

“Your audience should understand that whether the apprehending policeman takes a day or a month to capture his uh--person, his arrival time back here will still be the same. The ship’s Captain could change it, but there would be no point.”

The reporter gestured toward a digital clock that was counting down. “And that’s the time he gets here? Pretty soon, huh? But how do we know that Officer Krajan will be onboard? The Bee's never been used by a lone Police Officer before, has it?"

"No, and the Bee can't go large distances or go to new time locations beyond ten minutes without a passenger, so if Krajan left, Krajan will have to bring it back."

"Did he report capturing Spero 235?"

"Well, there's no way to send a message, but I'm told this apprehender is the best man on the force…" He held up his hand. "Wait, I'm getting an indication of orbital insertion."

The reporter backed away and motioned for cameras to focus on the Chief of Police sitting in as the ground commander. A computer voice came over the speakers. "Bee 77 requesting arrival at CD port, station one."

The Chief grabbed his microphone with a grin. "Krajan, switch to voice. Did you get him?"

"Uh--is this the landing bay talking?"

"Who the (expletive!!) are you? Put Krajan on."

"Uh, I'm Gary 250 from maintenance. No one else is in here with me. Can I come down now?"

The Chief stood up, slammed back against the Clean Room wall, and stared at his screen. His jaw was limp with disbelief, and his jowls started to tremble.

He wheeled to one side and pointed at a technician. "*You!* Take over. Bring him in." He snarled at one of his men nearby. "*You*, find out who this man is." To another, "And *you*--you assemble a reception team. No shooting. Take him to interrogation. No, wait. I'll talk to him myself right here."

The news team had backed away several paces, but the reporter moved in front of his camera and spoke in a whisper. "You're seeing this live, folks. Clearly something has happened to the Police Apprehender. I'm being told by our sources that this man, Gary 250, is someone on our outside maintenance crew. The mystery is how he replaced…"

The Chief suddenly remembered the cameras and a bellowing roar rose up in his throat. "Shut that thing off *now*. No more interviews." His men grabbed the camera lenses and pushed the crew toward the exits. "All you media people *get out*, all of you right *now*. Get out!"

Meanwhile in Saunders, Paul and friends were watching the live feed and laughing. "Wow, did you see the Chief's face when Gary came on?"

"But without TV there's no coverage," Susan said. "They'll just make up any cover story they want."

Paul turned toward her with a twinkle in his eyes. "Not this time we hope, my dear Susan. Justin had us place a really tiny surveillance cam in the Clean Room. We won't send its signal out yet or they'll be told about it and stop talking." He turned on a second view screen. "If this works, though, we can watch the Bee arrival right here, and we'll record everything for later broadcast."

A black and white, slightly grainy image of the empty arrival room appeared from a ceiling viewpoint. Paul continued, "This is a *very* small button camera. No frills, but it escaped detection, and they can't re-sweep for it in the vacuum chamber."

A glowing ball appeared in the room followed by a flash and a bang. The screen went blank. "No, *no*." Paul cried as he tapped the side of the monitor. After a few moments, static appeared and morphed into the image of a silver ovoid. "Ah, thank God. We weren't sure how our camera would take it when the sub-atomics snapped off."

Protesting men in white suits were shoved aside at the clean room door by the Chief and four of his soldiers. They rushed in toward the smoking, shiny Bee with guns drawn, and crouched down in firing position as the hatch opened.

Gary poked his head out. “You’re not gonna shoot me or anything, are you? I didn’t do anything wrong.”

The Chief held up his hand and the soldiers lifted their weapons up to forty five degrees. “Anyone else inside?”

“No Sir. Just me, Sir.”

“Get out slowly. Raise your hands.”

Gary backed out. He was wearing his maintenance coveralls and holding a folder in one hand. An officer grabbed him by the back of the neck, spun him around, and pushed him against the cold, steaming Bee. The other one took the folder. “Spread ‘em.”

“Ouch! It’s too cold to touch. What’s happening?”

Watching from Saunders, Susan mumbled. “He’s still groggy from the memory wipe. I sure hope he gets the story right.”

“All right then. Sit on the floor.” The Chief’s pasty-white jowls shook as he barked the orders. He turned to one of his soldiers. “OK, get some chairs in here and secure the view ports. This could be the only place in this weird building where no one can hear us.”

Gary sat surrounded by the police soldiers looking down at him. “Am I under arrest, sir?”

The Chief ignored Gary and spoke to the man next to him. “We’re not going to head quarters yet. Send for our police computer expert. I want him into this Bee ASAP. We’ll need all the data removed and secured.”

The Chief’s assistant dragged in some chairs but he glowered at the QDT techs who had come in and were standing along the wall in their Clean Suits. “You guys aren’t getting near this. Get out.” The Chief posted guards at the door, and paced around the room swearing.

Gary sat on the floor like a cross-legged child, with furtive glances around the room. The Chief let out a deep breath and seated himself in front of Gary. He took the folder from the soldier, glanced at it, dropped it on the floor with a pained smile, and lowered his copious eyebrows. “If you’re innocent, Gary 250, no one is going to hurt you, but we expect the truth. I’m sure you’ve something interesting to tell us?”

Gary looked up at the stern police faces staring down at him. “I—I, well I was dragging these branches you see. I had just cut them. They were touching the Dome you see, scratching the glass and…”

“Gary?”

"Yes, well this man in a uniform walked out of the woods with a gun. He motioned for me to come with him. Didn't talk. Well, I had no choice, you see."

"When was that?"

"I don't know. Well, wait. I was working on a Tuesday. Then we traveled a few days. Is it Sunday now?"

"Wednesday, the sixth."

"Really. So we actually came back the next day? How's that work?"

"Keep talking, Gary."

"OK, well he walks me down the hill, about half a K, and there's this glowing Bee just sitting there behind some rocks. Makes me get in with him."

"Did you ask him who he was?"

"Sure, but he didn't answer. The computer explained it to me--the one inside the Bee. He was from two thousand nine and didn't speak our language."

Susan crowded in to peer at Paul's monitor with John standing behind. "Gary's doing a great job, but he didn't have much time to rehearse this. What happens when they use a memory probe?"

John answered, "Well he won't remember Melissa, and Anna's team acted this out for him. It's amazing but they transferred a vid into his memory cortex. It's actually in there. The rest is just Gary, but he must be scared, huh?"

Paul held up his hand for silence when the Chief moved his chair closer and grabbed Gary's shoulder.

"Let's just skip to the part about what happened to my Agent Krajan."

"Uh--well Sir, the man from the twenty first century said he was an Ohio State Trouper. Once we got into the Bee it translated for us. He told me they caught him torturing Professor Main for information, but apparently the professor got out a call for help. When the local police came, Krajan started shooting. One of their men was killed."

"Sounds like self-defense. Why didn't they send Krajan back here?"

Gary tried to pick up the folder on the floor but a police guard kicked his hand and growled: "He asked you a question."

"Well--I, I guess it's not their way. Those papers explain his indictment. They said the trial for murder is quick, especially when a policeman is shot."

"So he's probably dead already. And they sent an officer back here just to tell us that?"

Gary twisted around in his chair. “Yeah, well, he said Krajan was yelling that the Bee would go nuclear and kill everyone if he didn’t get it back. They thought he just wanted to escape, but one of their people got inside and talked to the onboard.”

“The Connie program?”

“I don’t know. The computer anyway, but it confirmed the destruction process and how it could be avoided.”

The Chief stood up and began pacing back and forth in half circles around the Bee. “Well, that’s true of course, and the program would say there’d be no problem if someone brought it back.”

“I guess, and they were very angry about us interfering with their time, and…” He pointed to the floor. “Those papers tell all about it. Basically they say please don’t come back, especially with criminals, or else.”

The Chief stopped pacing and stared at Gary. “Or else, huh?” His voice became soft. “No one is going to tell us what to do.”

“But Sir, isn’t what you did against our laws anyway?”

“Shut up!” The Chief resumed pacing. “Why didn’t they land in the Dome? The onboard is programmed to do that.”

“Well, Sir, as the only passenger, he was acting Captain so he must have requested a stealth landing near the Dome.”

In Saunders, Paul grabbed the table edge. “Oh no! Is he going to tell him about our landing spot?”

“The onboard told me it made a low angle approach or something and stayed out of sight. He didn’t want to risk being captured himself. After what happened they don’t trust us, so he grabbed me and got out of there quickly.”

The Chief looked at his aide. “So now you see why external electronic sensors aren’t a waste of time. Turn them back on.” He stopped pacing in front of Gary. “And what do you think of this person who kidnapped you at gunpoint?”

“Well Sir, I thought he was very nice.”

He shouted: “*Nice?*”

“Yes, all of them. You’d have thought they’d take all this future technology we weren’t supposed to show them, but they took great pains to return everything even things that were evidence in their case. Krajan’s stunners are still there in the Bee.”

"OK, I've heard enough for now. Take him to police isolation."

"You want him to have an accident, Chief?"

Gary flinched and looked back toward the Chief as the two men grabbed him, but the Chief said, "Nah, the whole world knows about him. We'll just have to mess up his memory a little."

They dragged Gary off toward the door, and Paul turned away from his monitor with a grin. "World Media is still broadcasting live. They're doing interviews with people at the QDT. We're going to stream in the portion we just recorded. It will go out worldwide. Even if Administration shuts down every communication satellite, the broadcast will continue through our encrypted sideband on the weather satellite. They'll never figure out how we did it in time to stop us. This is one event the whole world will know about."

ANGER

Make certain that the government will belong to the people, not the people to the government.

Bernard M. Baruch, Princeton, May 1964.

"Time to take a break, Director." The message flashed on Justin's screen. It was the code for an urgent basement lounge conference.

Paul sat at a snack table by himself. His eyes were bloodshot and vertical wrinkles ran down below them. *A bit extreme for a forty-five year old man,* Justin thought.

"This must be about last night's newscast, right Paul? I saw people milling around the streets near the Police Building, angry people."

Paul motioned for him to take a seat. "Oh yes. Our addition to the broadcast that showed police in action had the same effect as an explosion. You and I will fondly remember what even relatively free media coverage once looked like. Actually we won't be seeing vid coverage of *any* kind now, except when Aten talks, and he's on tonight."

"The public needed to know the truth, Paul."

"They won't be getting *any* more truth from now on. And our sources tell us that what's happening here with people in the street is taking place in every single city Dome on the planet."

Justin pulled up a stool opposite Paul. "Do you think it was too much to add in the vids of the earlier police murders as well? Now everyone has witnessed those past atrocities, but now they know yesterday was no fluke. What else can the administration do? Faced with the will of the people, they'll be forced to prosecute the guilty and apologize."

Paul placed both arms on the table, exhaled loudly and looked intently at Justin. "My friend, my Boss, and we hope our leader, are you really that naive?"

"But any government has to change when the vast majority demand it. With the clips of Krajan's beatings and murders, they have to at least be open to dialogue."

"Apparently not their plan, Justin. You should understand that 'the will of the people' is simply an inconvenience to Aten's forces. Two air cars full of troops from the Supreme Directorate arrived in every city this morning. These guys went into every news office, arrested every single senior editor, and then proceeded to smash every bit of broadcasting equipment with large hammers. Is their mindset becoming clear?"

"Uh, oh. So much for fair and balanced reporting."

"This isn't funny, Justin. They are up on our Dome cutting off the antennas as we speak, and there are protesters shouting outside both the Police and the Chairman's buildings. If someone gets too carried away, I'm afraid we'll see shooting next."

"But Paul, if no one can get any news, they'd only be hurting themselves."

"The Police and weather antennae are spared, and at least that's good news since we depend on the weather band for our secret communications. But there'll be no independent news or entertainment programs, not even their crummy canned music. One way messages from the SD are all we're going to get."

Justin retrieved a bottle of water from the wall cooler, and walked around the room slurping at intervals. "Well, both sides are letting out their anger. Maybe that's a good thing for now. Perhaps it will lead to sitting down and discussing real changes. Any word on what they did with Gary?"

"They sent him in an air car to the SD for interrogation along with the editors, and some of your QDT techs. They're hoping to find out who is behind our video."

"As long as Gary's selective memory wipe holds, we're OK. The TV people and techs know nothing."

"Justin, you still don't get it? Aten's really angry. No one is going to negotiate, and revenge's coming our way. I can feel it."

"I do get it, Paul. The soldiers might well over-react, and Aten may be on the verge of a psychotic break down. OK, so I should start to worry about our protesters, particularly since I encouraged them. But without them we can't force negotiations, and I haven't given up on that idea. No one's been hurt yet, have they?"

"So far it's been just noisy and the Police seem to be ignoring everyone. On the other hand, they may be simply holding off on retaliation until all the broadcast equipment's destroyed."

Justin put the water bottle on the table and scratched his head. "Paul, this is just reactive anger and it should cool off in time. Is there anyone trying to organize the people on the street?"

"We have observers, but there's no one telling the protesters what to do or not to do. They're both ordinary people and Humwa mixed together, and that's nice, isn't it? But if there's anyone they *might* listen to, it would be you, Justin. You've still got hero status, my friend."

"Well, my advice for them would be to not get too close to the police sold--what's that buzz?"

"Someone's coming."

A fortyish, plump, dark-haired woman waggled through the door in a distraught rush. "Thank goodness you're here Paul. They said you'd be…" Suddenly she noticed Justin, realized she was out of breath, and collapsed on the couch. "Oh, Mister Director, I don't think we've actually met." She quickly extended a moist hand to Justin who had come over to help her. "I'm Monika 509 from Archives." She panted and tapped her chest. "Came as quickly as I could."

Paul added: "She's one of our observers."

Justin patted her hand. "My pleasure Monica. Do you have something of interest to tell us?"

"Oh, Sir…" She plucked out a mini-cam from her hair. "It's just awful. Wait till you see."

Paul plugged it into a wall monitor. It started with a view of the Police Headquarters as seen from a building across the street. The protestors were bouncing up and down and chanting: "Resign, Chief, Resign, Chief. Thou shalt not kill. Thou shalt not kill."

Twelve people rushed up the steps to the main entrance and began pounding on the large doors. Justin said, "Uh Oh. That's what I was going to warn against."

A side door opened and four soldiers with riot shields jogged out, shouted at them, demanding they leave, or else. They only retreated down a few steps.

Monika pointed to the middle soldier who was holding a device in his hand. "Watch this part. Sorry I didn't get a close up." A sudden screeching nose blasted from the screen, and all the people on the steps collapsed. Farther away in the street, protestors were kneeling and holding their heads. Officers began to pouring out of both the side doors, and the people in the street who were still conscious began to limp away, hands still on their ears. Paul paused the vid.

"When was this, Monika?"

“Just happened, Paul. An awful noise. You couldn’t hear it down here? But watch, it gets worse.”

The police soldiers stood on the top steps. They looked around, and waited for everyone to disperse. Then the officer holding the box gave a signal, and a cart wheeled out of the building. The bodies lying on the steps were hauled up to it and thrown in on top of one another like corn sacks. The cart containing the fallen bodies was pushed back into the building, and the vid ended with an empty square.

Monika stood up and looked desperately at the two stunned men. “They’re dead aren’t they? Dead!” Paul and Justin embraced the now sobbing Monika. “My friend Lisa was down there. I think she might have been one of those going up the steps. Paul, I have to go over to her place now and find out if she got back home OK.”

Paul patted her back. “We pray she did, but you go ahead, Monika. We’re going to send your recording to the science lab. A sound that kills? I hope they’re just unconscious.” Justin’s voice was hoarse. “Paul, if I’m really in charge, get the word out to all Humwa worldwide and anyone else who’ll listen. Stop these protests everywhere. Tell them--my *orders*.”

JERUSALEM

I will give power to my two witnesses

And they will prophesy… Rev: 11,3

"Levi Sir, reporting as ordered. He's up there again, flew in on an Air Car this morning."

Levi threw his head back and pushed away from his desk. He worked his fingers through salty black hair and squinted up at his messenger. "Good work. The Resistance needs to know, but how can you be sure it's him, Seth? They have the whole Temple Mount roped off—been that way for three years now."

"I got into that broken minaret on the opposite hill. The stone stairs are still there, and we have a peep hole for a telescope. Sir, I assume this office is bug free?"

"Yep, got another one of those things out of here this morning." He chuckled. "This little spy was in the *doorknob* if you can believe it, and was partly shielded too. If they get any more inventive they'll become Creative Humwa like us." Levi got up, hobbled to the window with a cane, and surveyed the view of Jeru Dome. "So talk, son."

"I don't think they are doing archeology, Sir. They're building something—something big."

"Seth, as far as anyone knows, this is the only place Aten ever visits outside of his Supreme Directorate, and he wants to keep it a secret. Why do you suppose that's true?"

"I don't know, but it's rumored he goes to Geneva Dome every few years too."

"Perhaps, but what's that abomination doing on the Temple Mount right now? That's the real question." Levi looked down at the street below and mumbled something about Police Troopers being everywhere. "Seth--this building--tell me: is it round?"

"Oh, you suppose he's rebuilding the mosque? Well, I don't think so. They cleared the top layers off and put in a foundation and walls. It's rectangular, and it sits on top of a buried foundation a little to the side of where the mosque used to be."

Levi turned to Seth, dark eyebrows lowered. “The Holy of Holies. They’ve found it. And can you tell what Aten is *doing* when he’s up there?”

“It looks like he just supervises. Of course he thinks he’s a god, right? He sits up high on a stone block that’s been covered with gold and white fabric. He’s got some carved poles stuck in the ground around him, and he’s wearing his tall headpiece with the sun-moon icons.”

Seth waited for Levi to respond, but he was looking out the window again. “Sir, if I may—what happened to the people at Home Synagogue Four, the one the police raided last week.”

Levi placed his hands on the windowsill and slowly leaned forward eyes closed until his forehead touched the glass. He spoke just above a whisper. “I’m sure they’re all dead, Seth.”

He gently rapped on the window with his head. “My wife’s brother was one of them, too.” He turned to face the young student, stood up fully, and pulled his shoulders back. “They hope to frighten us, hoping we’ll begin to obey without question. Don’t you see my son?”

“I’m sorry. I didn’t realize, but Aten’s never been able to kill our strange ‘Wise Men’, I know that. Troopers shot one of them this morning, but they still got away.”

“Our prophets from the desert? I had not heard.”

“Yes, the ones who walk around in brown patched up robes and preach about the Lord’s great victory. They talk about ‘Yeshua ha Meshach’. Aten might be able to kill us anytime he wishes, but not *them*. The trooper who shot him was burned up in *flames*.” “Flames from the prophet?”

“Our witness said so, but the police report says his weapon misfired. Sir, when will all this killing stop?”

Levi took a few steps toward him, his eyes rheumy. “There are things far worse than death, my friend. But you didn’t tell me. Does Aten hold anything in his hand?”

“Oh, yes Sir. It’s probably just a walking stick. He has a pole with his fancy gold sun ball on the top.”

Levi quickly stepped back; his eyes became wide.

Seth studied his expression. “That’s not important, is it?” “It is not a good thing, Seth.”

ATEN

On the top floor of the Chairman's building, Margo waited alone in the dim quiet of her secure message center where she had been summoned. She chewed on her thumbnail. The Police Chief sat in a similar room at his head quarters. They waited for the private broadcast from Aten himself.

The Supreme Directorate Colonel in charge of the newly arrived forces stood behind the Chief of Police and displayed no visible emotion. His erect, motionless pose resembled a bronze statue, honoring perhaps, no one but himself. Margo sat alone. She began to scratch her forearm.

Aten had informed his appointed leaders earlier by way of an encrypted message that he would address them an hour before his worldwide broadcast. A warning appeared on their screens: "The following message may only be viewed by my Elect, the Chairmen, and the Police Chiefs. Should *anyone* else be present, or if surveillance is suspected, terminate this broadcast and send notification."

The Colonel took out his badge and placed it on the table next to the Chief. He was one of The Elect.

A gong sounded, followed by a minute of silence. They were expected to attain the state of reverent submission. Aten's face filled the screen. A round, blue and gold helmet almost encircled his deeply tanned face, and his eyes were lined with black streaks drawn to points at his temples. The corner of his mouth drew back on one side as he spoke in a measured, resonant monotone. Aten did not smile.

"You have all failed on several occasions to carry out my orders. You have allowed my people to mistrust my rule." He stared silently at the camera with narrowed eyes as though he expected a reply.

The image pulled back slightly and he raised a jeweled scepter towards his audience. A resplendent golden sun with a scarab icon glittered on its top. "Even more serious is the penetration of our media by rebel Humwa. You forced me to witness the coverage of yet *another* disastrous Bee landing, one that mocked us.

Since you appear to be unable to anticipate, and are clearly incompetent at stopping these horrors, I ordered the cessation of *all* public media."

Aten glowered into the camera at his appointees. His head began to twitch rhythmically. His lids narrowed again, but suddenly his eyes burst open with a flash of flame. “At this time I am ordering sovereign law. There will be *no* general television, *no* printing, and a curfew at nine until you can *guarantee* that I will be free from meddling interference.”

The camera pulled farther back and showed Aten seated on his throne. He banged his scepter on the floor. “I *will* see vastly increased numbers at the morning and evening Thanksgiving Services for the gods. Do not apply physical force to accomplish this. You have other means.”

Aten raised his scepter over his head. “The troops of my Elect have sealed orders to deal with these rebel protestors. You are ordered to do what they ask.” All screens went blank.

# # #

The people of the world waited impatiently in every city dome, forced to crowd into the streets to hear their leader. All the world’s domes began to grind noisily as they closed above their heads. Citizens turned anxious, expectant eyes up toward the new government screens. Personal video for the population had ceased. Now there would only be official announcements, and the words of Aten would be viewed outdoors. The officers of The Elect observed the audience from elevated platforms beneath the screens in every city. One soldier held a black box.

Six minutes past the hour the World Anthem began to play, and the logo of The New World Order appeared on the great screens, a resplendent golden sun cupped by a crescent moon. The logo dissolved into Aten's full image. Shot from a low camera angle, he appeared to be a towering above them. Clothed in a purple and white robe, the gold edging on his blue helmet flashed in the spotlight with his every movement.

Paul stood next to Sarah and Justin on the sidewalk outside the QDT. Sarah nudged Justin. "That blue helmet really doesn't go very well with the purple, does it?"

Paul touched her shoulder. "Sarah, I've been told this round one is his Battle Helmet."

Aten looked down on his people. Electronically altered to make it deeper, his voice had a slight echo. "Democratic Partners, your behavior over the past few days has caused me, your leader and *The Aten* as well, much sadness. Surely you now realize that the broadcast you saw was another crude fabrication made by a few rebellious

Humwa. They have been dealt with, and in the future you will not be subject to their disturbing propaganda. I ask you now to forget this fiction the Humwa forced you to watch."

Justin whispered to Sarah. "Forget *all* TV now that they've smashed equipment."

Aten leaned back and surprised them with a slight smile. "Nine decades ago my grandfather ushered in a peaceful New World Order for our planet. Since then, even--even *Humwa* have enjoyed food, shelter, and health from our kindness. You have also been granted freedom from war, an earlier problem instigated by the Humwa."

He exhaled a breath and slowly shook his head. "Now it seems that some of you would like to make the Humwa equal to yourselves. With renewed power, these people would destroy our world again, so this I will not allow. However, I am merciful. Any Dome that chooses, may now allow the Humwa to vote for their representative, but the Humwa themselves may not hold such office."

Justin chuckled. "But since he still appoints the majority of representatives, he's lost nothing. Some compromise."

Aten made a sweeping gesture with one arm. The golden threads on his sleeve rippled and sparkled in the spotlight. "I require all of you to remain calm. You will find more joy in submission than rebellion. Some malcontents have fled into the wilderness, perhaps never to return. Our glorious Sun God is saddened by their loss, and our Moon God weeps at their foolishness."

Sarah tightened her grip on Justin's arm. "Oh Lord, he really did kill all those people, didn't he?" Justin nodded grimly.

The camera zoomed in, and Aten's face filled the screen. The black lines drawn around his eyes drew together in a squint. "I will expect no more street protesting or secret meetings. This belief in an unseen God and your meetings to worship him are repugnant to me. They will stop. They will *stop!*"

A blazing sun appeared behind Aten. "Instead my people will go at eight in the morning and eight in the evening to worship gods you can see, the *only* true gods." He raised his arms overhead. "The morning tranquility heralds The Aten, the god of our light. Ilah, the god of our moon will watch over you by night."

The camera pulled back and showed him relaxing back in his golden chair, displaying a full and beatific smile. "I, Aten am your god's representative on this planet. My mercy is great, but know that it is not without limit. Go now. Renew your faith in my protection, increase your work production with joy, and give thanks to the gods who give our Earth all things."The screens around the world went black, but a moment later, one sentence appeared as the world stared in silent shock.

"There will be no third chance."

FAITH

All the universe contains regularities known as symmetries. These permit physicists to describe it mathematically, but no one knows why. Marco Liveo, theoretical astrophysicist: Scientific American, August, 2011.

Reverend Billy paused and smoothed back his silvery hair. He had reached the closing lines of his sermon at Saunders' Christian service. "In these very troubled times when we may face death itself, we must learn to trust our human abilities less, and trust our God more--much more."

He grasped the lectern with both hands, his face anguished. He searched the eyes of each congregant one at a time. "I *know* how you feel about our fallen, but know that their deaths—their deaths will one day be swallowed up in the Lord's *victory*. I want to hear an Amen." Earnest "Amens" resounded.

"As you know they have disabled the print function on all computers. Since most of you do not have bibles, our volunteers have made hand written copies of Matthew 14:27-31, the 23rd Psalm, and First Corinthians 15:54-55 for you. Please pick them out by the door as you leave."

Billy walked down to the front row and raised his right hand over the people. "May Jesus be your guide and protect you, and may His Spirit remain with you always." They answered: "And also with you. Amen."

The congregation began filing out, and he called over them. "Oh, and people, brother Paul has an encrypted bible you can download on your Hand-Helds if you want to risk it. And remember, for those of you who do not have to get back into the Dome right now, there is going to be a brief special meeting with the other God Groups right here. Leave the doors open and welcome them as they arrive."

Many believers who were not on duty in the Dome began to file in. They included Jews, "The Eucharists", "The Children of God", the "Returned Children of Abraham" or RCAs as they were called, "The Waters of Life", and others. Reverend Billy's flock simply called themselves "The Christians", and at the moment they were busy embracing everyone who walked in.

The leaders of the other God Groups assembled at a long table set up on the stage. Their mood was somber. Billy introduced each of them, and addressed the audience. “Welcome everyone to our council of minds and spirits. As reports filter in from around the world, it’s clear that we’re facing a world crisis not seen in over a hundred years.”

He strode over to the lectern. “But let me open with one note of encouragement. For the first time we actually *have* reports coming in from the rest of the world. Paul Anderson has just established a communication link with every other City, and it remains undetected by Administration. And you will be happy to learn that every Dome reports the presence of dozens of secret congregations like our own, and their followers are growing. Preliminary numbers estimate that perhaps two out of every three citizens meet in secret God gatherings. The Holy Spirit is doing a mighty work.”

A red cheeked woman in the front row waved her arms. “Billy, lets just get to the ‘how we gonna fight’ part.”

A commotion followed and Billy motioned for quiet. “All right. All right. I feel the best answer is to take a calm look at our situation and our options. When the majority of people want to change a government ruled by an undesirable person, they have several choices. In a Democratic Republic they just vote new leaders. In some, pressure on and from influential people like Business leaders or Bankers can cause change. These options do not seem to be available to…"

A heavy set man in maintenance coveralls was leaning in the side wall. "So there's nothing left but war, right?"

Billy flashed him a stern look. "So we Humwa would become what they say we are? I was going to add general peaceful demonstrations before we consider last resorts."

A pastor on his right cleared his throat. "Jim McClure, Eucharists. You've heard about the murder of one of our priests, and arrest of nine people. Right now the troops seem to be able to disperse our demonstrations and even kill us in mass numbers. They have some new weapon and just dropped a dozen protestors, one of them was a pregnant woman from our congregation. Street fighting does not seem to be an option."

A woman leader spoke out. "And we're still waiting to hear about the fate of those poor people."

"Most likely *killed!"* came out of the audience.

Another minister turned to Billy. “Has anyone considered a general work stoppage? It would be a safer way to demonstrate that people hold the final power.”

Jacob, the Jewish leader, raised his hand to speak. ”I can answer that. A general strike would only lead to our having no goods or services and collective world misery for everyone, except of course at the SD. Aten would laugh at us.”

Caleb from Waters of Life raised his hand. “But what if, instead of demonstrations, we have worldwide public worship in the streets, praying hand in hand. All people united, trusting in God, and unafraid to show our belief.”

When audience applause to this died down, Jacob stood. “All of us here would love to see that, but it would only lead to a more massive extermination. We Jews understand this. Executions happen every day in Jeru Dome because Aten has absolutely *no* compassion for human life.” He threw his arms up and sat down.

Billy turned to him and spoke over the murmuring. “Jacob, anything more?”

“No, Billy. But remember, Justin has requested we hold off on any street gatherings until they determine what really happened when those people fell. I do know this: now is the time to run *to* the God of Abraham and Moses, *not* from Him. Only He can protect His faithful from this abomination."

Jacob mopped his balding brow, looked at Caleb, and smiled. "I met with Caleb and Billy earlier today. After some disagreements, we hugged a lot, and cried a lot." He paused, and mopped his eyes. "Oh sure, we've often argued about some things. But in the presence of God's uniting and awesome love, I assure you: today we are one people."

Caleb nodded his head. "And we will be, must be, always." His expression brightened. "And here's an example of Holy Spirit power. The smartest guy on the SD enforcement squad, the one that recently crushed two God groups, came to know the Lord last week. And I mean big time and on fire. Name's Mujir. Now he is actively protecting us, and we all hope he can keep his cover."

"Praise God" rang out with much hand waving. Billy raised his hand. "Pay attention to Justin's order, though. I don't want any of you out there in the streets testing your promise of eternal life. You hear?"

Jacob waved his cloth at the people. "Yes, yes, our lives are precious to us and to Him. Let's use them wisely."

Caleb stood and raised his arms. "I should mention one other thing to all of you. Sarah, one of our members, is a prophetess. She had a vision of many more lives being lost on Earth, but she *also* saw God restoring the faithful. She saw His laws being written on our hearts, and peace prevailing for a millennium. In short, her prophesy is that our Lord will ultimately be victorious."

The audience became restless again. "Well then, how about *our* victory plan, then?" the ruddy woman shouted. "Maybe that means we *should* fight."

A slender pale arm went up and received a nod from Billy. "Rebecca, Children of God." She smiled at the woman. "It is perfectly clear that we are physically powerless. We have no political, financial, or military means of defense against this demonized man and his system whose purpose is to turn us away from God. But remember Psalm 32. 'You will protect me from trouble and surround me with songs of deliverance.' We must turn toward God now as Jacob said, for without His help our cause is, and always will be, without hope."

Reverend Billy stood, and motioned to silence the murmurings. "So to answer the question about our plan: for now at least, the plan is to be patient."

The shouter called, "So there really *is* no plan."

"The plan is also for us to use the most powerful weapon we earthly humans have, and that is prayer. Pray today for Justin and his team who are fighting for us and the answers we need right now. Pray for our people living in persecution, and the families who have lost loved ones. Pray for Jerusalem so the Holy City will be free once more. Pray also for the very people who attack us that they may be enlightened. But especially, I want you to pray for our deliverance."

This time the room remained quiet. All said "Amen."

RESPONSIBILITIES

A week after Aten's pronouncements, Justin was alone in his apartment pacing from living room to kitchen trying to keep his thoughts on plans for the next Bee design. However, nagging thoughts about Aten's increased stranglehold on one hand, and daydreams of Sarah filled his mind. He was ecstatic that she had accepted his marriage proposal right away and with a big happy grin too. They had decided their special day would be on the last day of summer, not that far away.

Justin's reverie came to an abrupt halt with a knock on his door. No request from the front gate, no door signal, just a knock. Unusual. Cautiously he peered at the door vid. A short, dark skinned person stood outside facing away, but the metal scan was negative. He shrugged his shoulders and opened up.

John's fourteen year old boy stood in front of him with a gleaming white grin and one finger over his lips. Without speaking the boy turned an erasable pad toward him. It bore the words: "Meeting in one hour, 12 Malthus Court. Can you attend?"

Justin nodded. He struggled to remember the boy's name. *I think it's Tony.* The boy held up a hand, signaling him to wait. Tony went a few steps down the hall and came back with one of Paul's sending devices for implant locator beacons. He put the little yellow box down just inside his door and flipped the switch. Justin felt the startling click in his head. *I still like Anna's method better.*

Tony wrote another message. "Side stairway, service exit. Take the long way. Jog." He grinned again and waved good bye.

# # #

Justin picked a zigzag route through the city. He swung around one corner and saw a group of people herded against a wall by police troupers. He jogged away crossing the street while the police disgorged obscenities at the frightened citizens.

Finally he trotted up to the address and found himself standing in front of an apartment building. *Darn. Tony forgot to give me the apartment number*. But as he approached the side exit door it buzzed open and Anna's grin welcomed him. "Hi Boss, follow me."

Sarah appeared from a side corridor and danced up to him, sparkly faced. Justin glanced toward Anna and held up his hand. "A moment." With their wedding only weeks away, a brief but lingering kiss was an imperative.

Anna giggled. She led them down a stairway, opened a locked steel door with her handprint, and showed them to a basement apartment. "This is one of the secure spots used for God Meetings and there's one going on right now. Should be over soon, but we can go in and watch."

The living room furniture had been moved into a circle. Seven people faced one another including Paul and John. A foldable wooden cross sat upright on a coffee table in the center, and a heavy set woman stood talking to the group. "It's an abomination." She gestured for emphasis. "It's against every moral and common sense principal not to mention the will of our Lord…"

She noticed the others coming in, returned a welcome smile, and motioned toward chairs along the wall.

The woman smoothed her dress out and sighed. "We have to find some way to put an end to this." She pointed to a blonde woman. "Ruth, you have a fifteen year old daughter. In a matter of months she will be taken away from you and Bill forever. If you're 'lucky' the State will 'replace' her with a stranger from another city. How do you feel about that?"

Ruth took a tissue and blew her nose. "You know right well how every parent feels, Eva. But we would all become inbred if the State didn't do this, wouldn't we?"

"And that whole presumption smells like a sewage leak to me. There's five thousand young people in this Dome. Do they think they'll somehow illegally marry their siblings?"

Eva sat down but continued, her tone deliberate. "Our children are *our* responsibility. The Lord said so, and it's just common sense. Maybe if everyone could travel freely to any city, we wouldn't have to worry about so called inbreeding in the first place. As it is, you'll likely never speak to your daughter again. Not allowed."

John cleared his throat. "Unless you're an Elect. Everyone else only gets to see two cities: the one you're born in and the one you die in."

"Well, you're a Director. Can't you travel and see your older children?"

“Not even Directors, Eva. We’re not Aten’s Elect. We do get some Business Travel but only on an approved assignment. And it’s never approved if you have a child in the city you request. Actually that’s a hint at where your kid might be, but we just don’t get to go.”

“Well, there you have it: Satan’s plan to destroy the family. Let’s all do some thinking about a counter plan. Your handout has some Bible readings for next time.”

Paul raised his hand. ”Eva, there’s one group of people who’ve found a way to beat this nasty system.”

All eyes turned to him in open mouthed awe. “Of course what I’m going to tell you doesn’t leave this room.” He studied the amazed faces, and waited for head nods. “In Jeru Dome, the Jewish people have been keeping their families together for about seventy years now, but it costs them a lot.”

“What cost? How?” Ruth asked. “The ships come and take our kids away. They return with others to take their place. No one can change that.”

Paul said, “If this is spoken of on the outside you could destroy some of the families you want to save. Let me see a hand raised if you’ll keep this a secret even from your own families.”

Satisfied, he continued. "When the Domes were under construction, many wanted one where Israel had been. Those were the pre-Aten days, and even though there was considerable radiation and no remaining population in the area, a good number of surviving Jews came there from all around the world, some Christians too. Of course there were Jews who remained in the other Domes as well.

"According to Monika, our historian, Jeru Dome was built in the ruins of what had once been Jerusalem. It is next to the southern part of the old city wall on the remnants of a bus station and a garden."

Justin's brow furrowed. "But, with decades of children being dispersed every year, that ethnicity should all be lost by now."

Paul grinned. "That's the plan of our New World Order, isn't it? But for the last seventy years Jeru Dome has kept most of their families at home by working with the SD Police Transporters."

General laughter. Ruth said, "Those Police won't even *talk* to us much less take any risks for us."

"These drivers do talk to them. They're given the cash equivalent of two years earnings, and the drivers keep quiet about it. It's too good a thing for them to lose. Here's what happens. Onboard their Police aircar is a device to check the child's implant transponder code. But this device can *change* the code as well, so they change the code of the child from Jeru Dome to the code of the child who was scheduled to take his or her place.

These teenagers still go to the distribution center and get a new name to go with their new code but really it's the same child that left. No one at the SD has caught them yet."

Eva walked over to Paul with her eyes squinted. "But--but two *identical* codes?"

"Nope. The child who *would* have gone to Jeru has his or her codes switched too, and they go to wherever the Jewish child was going. The police driver also tells them that their taking on a new name is required and secret. It's all quick and painless. Remember, everyone has to be code checked by the machine."

But they wouldn't *look* any different."

"Right, and sometimes the child from Jeru gets minor plastic surgery on arrival so they also look more like the replacement."

John's large frame swiveled in his chair to face Paul. "But wait a second. Statistically once every twenty one times, the *other* child, the non Jewish child who was supposed to go to Jeru Dome, would end up right back with *his* parents too."

Paul laughed. "Yes, that's happened three times we know of. So far, not a single complaint. (laughter) Those parents get their own child back, and that's how we found out about it. Of course the parents need to practice calling him or her by the new name."

Eva put her hand on his shoulder. "I'm so glad that at least some families aren't torn apart, but how could anyone come up with two whole years of pay?"

"By saving for it since their childhood and keeping it all in cash. The Jews who returned last century were as devoted to God as anyone in this room is. And they *really* don't like losing their children--or their homeland."

Eva held onto Paul's shoulder. She looked around her living room at the others. "This gives us hope. Thanks, Paul. We have the same God, my friends, and while we may not be raising our own children, remember that we will always be one family." She raised both arms overhead. "May the Lord bless you all. May His spirit fill your hearts with joy, and may you always know His path."

"Amens" were heard around the room. Eva turned to Justin. "Most here will be leaving in a minute. Sorry to hold up your meeting. I know how important it is. I'll have fresh coffee for you in a moment."

# # #

John and Paul remained for their meeting and greeted Stephen 430, a neurosurgeon who appeared at the door with an apology for being late.

Justin smiled at Paul. "That was fascinating stuff about Jeru Dome. Are you the one who called this meeting?"

"Yes. We've analyzed how the mass attacks were accomplished, and I'm sorry to confirm that they *were* indeed murders. We're here to see if we can figure out a defense against their evil black boxes. Twenty-one cities have resistance groups like ours, but we've never had contact with Geneva Dome. The majority have formally asked Carolina Dome to be in charge of the resistance. And Justin, like it or not, we all want you to lead us. We trust you."

Justin felt a sudden rush, and a warmth from the faces intently focused on his. He turned to his friend, John. "Well, I'm flattered, but tell me, why would all of you trust someone so new to your side?"

John's great head nodded. "*Because* Justin, Anna knows your mind, Sarah knows your heart, I know your friendship, and Paul knows your leadership."

Justin's head dropped, but a grin covered his face. His mind raced. *Can I refuse? Should I refuse?* He raised his head. "Can I put that in my resume? What can I say? I'll accept, of course. So what new information do you have for us, Paul?"

"First, and sadly, there were twenty three souls on the police steps who were murdered by Aten's soldiers that day. Our God Squads are out consoling the victim's friends and their families. Nine escaped and are recovering in their homes. You'll hear why they didn't die in a moment. Administration put all the survivors they could round up into the SD psychiatric building."

"Can't Susan see them?" Justin asked. "She's the Health Director, after all."

"Nope. They've been declared a menace to Dome safety. Besides, no one gets into that center anyway."

Justin sat down next to Sarah and gently massaged her shoulder when he realized she was crying. "How did they kill them, Paul? I've never seen anything like this."

Paul shrugged and shook his head. "It's our *implants*, people. Anna and Stephen have analyzed their response to the noise we recorded at the scene. These sound waves have a digital message coded in that triggers a reaction from all implants except the ones the police and the Elites are given. Apparently this was programmed into *all* our implants probably back to the first Aten. Even a ninety year old museum piece responded the same way."

"And the response is a nasty one," Stephen said. "If the sound is above a certain decibel level, all the charge in the power pack discharges into the brain, and one of the wires goes to the breathing center in the medulla. Just below the lethal sound level, there's only a partial discharge through a few of the wires. That's why those who are farther away from the sound are injured, but recover. The manual says the medulla wire is a health monitor, but now we understand its real purpose."

Sarah squeezed Justin's arm. "Oh God, so they can just kill *anyone* with a touch of a button? That's what Aten wants: absolute control over life and death."

Justin put his arm around Sarah's shoulders, and turned to face Anna. "I assume all of you here know about

Anna's secret abilities. Anna, what's different about this sound weapon and what you can do?"

Anna bounced up from her chair. "Oh, it's very different, Boss. All I do is send an impulse to turn off awareness. It's a short, quick unconsciousness. No one's hurt by it."

"Unless they're flying an air car?"

Anna laughed. "But there's some *good* news. Once Steve told me about this trigger in the implant, I practiced with one in the lab that wasn't implanted. It turns out that I can turn off the implant's response permanently if I can get close enough, say within a meter or so. I turned off this circuit in my own implant first, then I did it for each of you this evening when we said hello. You didn't feel a thing, right?"

"Our Anna," Paul gestured toward her as he faced the audience. "Now if we could only find a way for her to give the whole world a hug, and we'd hug back, wouldn't we?"

Anna spun around like a ballerina. "Well maybe there *is* a way, guys. I'm working on a software upgrade for Paul's implant relocator. He should be able to change anyone's implant vulnerability with his device just like I can."

"But here's our problem," Paul said. "Even if we get Anna's reprogramming to work in our machine, how would we ever be able to use it on the entire world population? We've only got five machines, and they're all here."

Justin stared at the ceiling in thought. After a moment his hands popped up. "Susan," he whispered.

"Susan?"

"Yes, Susan, our Director of Health, *and* Director of World Health too."

"Yes, but what could she do?"

Justin grinned. "Plenty. We're only a month or so away from our annual worldwide immunizations and checkups."

Anna chirped. "Of course, Boss. That's it. All we have to do is find a way to make the deprogrammer work with Susan's diagnostic equipment."

"And," Paul raised his index finger. "*And*--there's a Health Director's conference a week before the program starts. Every Director is supposed to bring in their equipment for software updates. Perhaps we can add a little update of our own. But remember, most of the World's Health Directors are not part of our resistance movement, so our device will have to function automatically."

Justin stood up with a grin. “This was Aten’s ultimate back up terror weapon, wasn’t it? If we can eliminate his advantage, we can be back out there protesting again. We’ll be a worldwide force, and we can take the world back.”

Paul stood up, his brows low. “Yeah, more than protest, we could start a new government. There are a lot of regular police on our side. They’ll give us access to weapons.”

Justin shook his head. “But hopefully we won’t have to overthrow the government by war. Aten may be evil, but we’ll finally be in a position to pressure him into giving us some rights, some *real* changes.”

Paul glanced around the room. “Justin, there’s a lot of us who do *not* want to compromise with Aten.”

Sarah stood up next to him, and slid her arm around his waist. “But this would be a peaceful way to try first. If everyone is free from this awful dread, perhaps the end of fear will be the first step towards freedom. Then perhaps we can begin to build this beautiful future world I’ve seen in my dreams.”

THE SUPREME DIRECTORATE

The coming of the lawless one will be in accordance with the work of Satan, displayed in counterfeit miracles and all sorts of evil. 2 Th: 2, 9.

Goren 660 tugged at his scarlet jacket and forced his shoulders back. He felt a wave of cold perspiration as the great golden doors slowly opened before him. The Royal Guardsman briskly stepped inside, bowed and announced: "Most Worshipful Aten: presenting Goren 660, Director of Intelligence."

Goren took a few shaky steps into the throne room. The smell of the incense made him dizzy. "I (cough) am at your service, your Worship. How can I please you today?"

Aten's public throne sat at the end of the corridor, two meters above the shiny cobalt floor. His voice echoed behind a high console surrounded by transparent panels.

"First:" He pointed to a sun medallion on the floor with a wave of his gold embroidered sleeve. "Stand there."

As Goren approached, he realized he was all alone in this long corridor-room with Aten. Unusual, he thought. His footsteps echoed on the Lapis tile. He saw no guards, but knew a whole garrison waited behind the back wall. No doubt they were watching. "Great One, I have sent complete intelligence reports. I fear there will be nothing more I can add today."

A clear panel slid to the side, and Aten's head tilted down to face him. On this day he wore a white turban bearing the emblem of a black scarab. "What an interesting thing for a gatherer of intelligence to say. Tell me, when you want to interrogate someone, do you just ask them to jot down a few notes for you?"

"Of course n—I see your point."

"Goren, you might think my most troublesome Dome is South Africa, but I'm most worried about Carolina. You have given me rumors that Justin 126 is a Humwa leader, and wielded some special power when the escaped Bee returned, but you offer no proof. From now on, do not trouble me with rumors. I want facts."

"Yes, Great One."

“You also make note that he is to marry the Chairman’s Receptionist. Has this person been under surveillance?”

“Of course, Your Worship, but we have no facts, only suspicions in her case.”

“Suspicions are more important than rumors. I will hear them.”

“My investigator believes she is a witch of the unseen God.”

Aten leaned forward, looked down at Goren, and smiled. “Now that, Goren, is amusing. Chairman Margo is faithful to me but has given me nothing but the best reports concerning her.”

“Her work is exemplary, but Sarah 202 definitely has a secret life.”

“Very well, Margo will discharge her, and your men will keep watch. I recall you have a soldier in her Dome who has located several secret groups.”

“Yes, your worship. That would be Mujir P94. He was recently honored by the Carolina Police Unit.”

Aten slid back into the comfort of his throne. “Well then, put him on it.”

“Yes, Great One.”

All right, Goren, let's move on to something that should be easy for you. Tell me about the missing body."

Goren stared up at Aten, speechless. He quickly reached for his palm tablet. Aten sighed, "Take your time. Take your time." He chuckled. "Oh here's a *hint*. Carolina Dome again, two months ago, name began with a P."

"Um, um, oh yes. You must mean Patricia 248, killed while obstructing justice?" He looked up, his face now full of pride. Aten just stared at him. He squinted at the tablet again. "Cremation remains were definitely received here at SD three days later."

"Goren, why is it we prefer whole bodies to ashes?"

"Because these are the unfaithful, and they are burned as an offering on Ilah's altar." He held up a finger and rechecked his data pad. "Oh, sorry. I see a footnote here that says the family got to the body first. They did the cremation, probably with a forged permission. We will investigate."

"This is a sacred rite, Goren. The smoke must rise to Ilah on the next full moon or she will be displeased."

"My apologies, Great One. I will make inquiry in Carolina Dome and send a report. The troublemaker you mentioned, Justin 126, is the Director in the building where this happened."

"Yes, and he might also be responsible for that disgusting pirate video seen around the world. He's become a local hero, I'm told. I don't enjoy heroes."

"Should he suffer an accident?"

Aten leaned back and pursed his lips. "Not yet. You have no hard evidence, remember? He does attend my morning services, and his department is productive. Besides, I will require him to give me a Bee capable of flying four people."

Goren checked his palm pad. "You will receive a report on him and his woman within the week."

Aten leaned forward, his eyes narrowed to slits. "Yes, double your surveillance. These two may be all the more dangerous together. And while you are *making inquiry* Goren, find out why the ashes we received for our ceremony, ashes marked 'Patricia 248', were actually those of chickens and *rodents*."

Goren staggered backward. "Oh—oh *my*. Yes, Great One. I will investigate--*fully* investigate."

Aten stared at him for several silent minutes. Goren, cleared his throat, shifted his weight, and studied the gold panels surrounding the murals. He was particularly interested in various head dresses hanging on the wall behind the throne. A bowel movement seemed imminent. Aten spoke in a soft voice. “Goren?”

“Yes, Great One?”

“Your report also states that our ‘Vermin Killer’ box has not been deployed anywhere in the world since its successful use at Carolina Dome. Is that correct?”

“Yes, Great One. It was *most* effective, and many people believe it came from your miraculous powers.” He grinned. “There have been *no* protests requiring its use since then.”

“But all communication between cities has been cut off. Do you find it strange that a single use of our killer box would immediately shut down protests *worldwide*?”

“Um, I see. You are so wise, Great One. Perhaps they *still* have some means of communication.”

Aten leaned forward, his smile beatific. “And I would think an *Intelligence* Director would find that especially interesting, don’t you think?”

“Yes, yes, of course I’ll look into it. That should have occurred to us.”

Aten shook his head. “It should have. And your report did not mention that we actually *had* another incident involving my so called miraculous device. I wish to know more about what happened at South India Dome. The Chief there reported the deployment of the Vermin Killer, but said it 'was not needed'. Unusual, don't you think? Apparently, the people ran away when they saw it. He gave no details."

"Yes, yes, of course. I'll get you a full report."

Aten leaned back with a sigh. "You may go Goren." The Director began the procedure of backing toward the door and bowing while trying to conceal his intestinal urges. "And I am sure you will provide us with *far* better service in the future."

"Yes, yes I *will*, Great One." He gave a final bow at the doorway.

Aten gave a final word with a grin. "Goren, not all of the smoke we offer up to Ilah comes from the Humwa."

DECEMBER 2247

Justin stood in awe at his apartment. He leaned against the door frame to take it in. Not only was his furniture rearranged again, but some of it was gone and replaced with new things. Where he used to see the back of his couch, he was greeted by a straight vista leading to his out door patio. New wall hangings seemed to be everywhere and one wall was now dark red.

My bachelor place has been attacked. I should be really annoyed right? But I'm loving this.

Justin grinned at the sound of Sarah, softly singing in the kitchen. "Hi, Dear. I got off work early today."

That's why.

Sarah skipped quickly around the corner wiping her hands on a dishrag. She tossed it on the floor and encircled her husband with kisses and hugs. She held his head with both hands, and her fingers wiggled into his hair. Justin felt giddy. Her eyes sparkled. "I hope you like the changes my darling. The paintings are my grandmother's."

"I just *love* it, darling. It will be like you're here even when your not. This must have taken you all day. But how come you hardly changed anything for the first few months we were married?"

She released Justin's head and turned to gesture at the living room. "I liked just feeling a part of you at first, but today it hit me: we're an "*us*". And of course it should be *our* place, so if you see something you don't like, just tell me."

She took his hand and led him out onto the patio, closed the slider and pointed. "Look at this. The leaves are gone from those trees and now you can see a distant mountain top even with the Dome closed."

Sarah leaned out on the railing. "But weren't those fall colors beautiful just a few months ago? From ground level inside the Dome, you can't see much at all."

"Justy, you didn't have *any* furniture on this porch." She gave him a curious squint, then giggled. "So I brought some from my old place. Course I had to get rid of a millimeter of dust and grime out here too. All right now, sit and put your feet up. I'll get us some snacks."

Justin shook his grinning head as he watched his wife bound back into the kitchen. He called out: “Don’t spoil me too much, dear. I’ll really turn out rotten.”

She returned with cheese, crackers, glasses, and a wine bottle. “Anna sent this wine to us. Completely contraband. Hope you like it. And don’t worry, you’re the one spoiling me.”

Justin struggled with the strange closure she called a cork, but finally he was able to pour some cherry red liquid into the glasses. “Delicious. Where does she get it? Are we celebrating something?”

“The Chairman’s Headquarters.” They clinked glasses. “I got fired today.”

“No! How could Margo do that to you? We’re celebrating?”

Sarah turned to Justin with a smile and a toss of her auburn hair. “Oh, don’t worry. I’m glad really. That’s one of the things we’re celebrating. I’m having fun doing some volunteer work, and fixing this place up with my free time.”

“I think I can guess the reason she let you go.”

“Margo said the Police have listed me as a security risk. She put it off for weeks, but said she had no choice, and was actually sweet about it if you can believe that.”

"Well I admit, I thought that might be coming. And I assume you got on that list because you're now married to the King of the underworld?"

Sarah laughed. "Something like that, but don't you worry. You're too useful and popular with the people. She'd never discharge you."

Justin took a sip of wine and put his glass down. "Maybe not until I deliver the new Bee. I just wish I could have seen Margo actually being nice."

"Well, she was, and she was apologetic, too. Asked me what I'd like for a late wedding present."

"This is getting more interesting by the second. We've been married over three months. What could you possibly ask her for?"

"I asked for the video and audio monitoring be removed from our bedroom and never be replaced."

Justin straightened up, his eyes wide. "No kidding."

"Yup. Said she was really horrified the police would have put it in there anyway, and she wrote a full executive order to stop it. John was just here to check it. The room's really clear, and so is this outdoor patio, by the way. I think John threw that in himself."

"So we can actually talk freely? Great. Well, I'm happy to tell you that the world immunization program is going well and it's almost complete."

"And has it been, uh, tested?"

Justin poured another wine-taste for each of them. "Let's save the rest for dinner, OK? Well, not really *tested,* except in the lab, but Paul passed on a little story from South India Dome I know you'll like."

Sarah twisted sideways in her seat, and slithered a bare foot into his lap for a massage. "Ooh, what?"

"The police don't know about the immunity yet, and I'll bet you've noticed more SD troupers out there. They brought several black killer boxes into every Dome."

"But why? Things have been really quiet lately."

"They're still getting ready for a possible revolt, and the SD's training local police. Anyway, that leads into my story. There was a protest with about twenty people outside the India Police Headquarters a few weeks ago. When they started up the steps, the SDs handed one of the boxes to a local policeman in riot gear."

Sarah shook her fingers. "I thought you ordered a stop to the protests. So they disobeyed. Well anyway, did the immunization work? Were any people killed?"

"Here's the part you'll like. The policeman refused to use the device and smashed it on the pavement. I don't think local police knew the box actually killed people until a few months ago."

"Oh, bless him. But what happened to the man?"

"Two of the SDs started clubbing him on the spot, but the local forces held them off. They fired warning shots in the air to keep the demonstrators away. Finally all the police went inside and dragged this guy in with them."

Justin was enjoying Sarah's rapt attention. He settled back and took another bite of cracker and cheese. "But, but," Sarah pulled her foot away and sat on the edge of the chair. "You must know something else. Is the poor man OK now or not? What did the protestors do?"

"Well, somehow the crowd got his badge name, Sean P340. They started chanting for him, chanting they'd go home if the SD released him."

"Well, well, did they?"

"It took about twenty minutes, but oh yeah. They tossed him out a side door in his underwear, no badge and no weapon. Obviously not on the force any more. He was bloodied up pretty badly, and he could hardly walk. Maybe the SDs thought the angry crowd would finish him off."

Sarah pounded her fists on Justin's knee. "Oh no. Oh, no, they *wouldn't* would they? He saved them. Tell me they didn't hurt the poor man."

"They didn't. In fact there was a lot of hugging and tears--like I see in your eyes right now." Justin grinned and wiped one of Sarah's tears with a napkin. "They took Sean to one of their homes and got him treated and cared for. The demonstration was over."

"Oh, that's a wonderful story, Justin. And Aten should get the message that our own police won't be ruthless and evil just because he orders them to do horrid things."

"I wish that were true for all our local police, but we still don't know if the immunization actually works." He sniffed the air. "What's that wonderful smell coming from my old bachelor kitchen?"

Sarah laughed. "I made some stew. It should simmer awhile longer. But first I want to show you a surprise in the bedroom."

Justin cocked his head to one side and put a finger in his cheek. "I think I've seen that surprise, dear."

Sarah let out a screech followed by a quick rib tickle attack. "No, you naughty man, not that." She lifted his arms and stood him up. "No comments until we're in our other bug free zone."

Justin found himself escorted back to his own bedroom. Sarah didn't turn on the lights until the door was closed. She sang "Ta-taaa," and flicked them on. Lighted multicolor lights were looped across every wall, and a beautifully decorated tree sparkled in the corner. "Merry Christmas, darling." She gave him a hug and a quick kiss.

Justin laughed and returned the kiss. "Merry, *completely forbidden,* Christmas to you too, my dear."

"But, isn't it *beautiful*? And no one will know if we keep it in here." Sarah did a little dance and twirled around the room.

"Where'd you get the lights?"

"They're hand colored—in a secret workshop somewhere." She landed on the edge of the bed with a bounce. "They're all so bright and colorful, aren't they darling? It makes me happy just to look at them."

It's really festive. I love it too, dear."

"It *is* a happy time, darling. It's to remind us that God is *really* here, and he loves us so much he sent his only Son to live and suffer with us. Save us too. And Christmas day is tomorrow, you know."

"Yes, and half the working people in the Dome take a sick day, the one and only time each year. And that really, *really* makes the Administrators angry. I remember how I used to hate it too."

"But now you don't, do you. Know why?"

"Cause suddenly I felt different inside about so many things, and it's not just because I love you and we're married."

Sarah patted the bed next to her so Justin would sit. Large, curious eyes worked their way into his. "Tell me about *different*, my love."

"Different. Well, after we were married in the Judicial Office, you took me to that God Meeting where I accepted Jesus as Lord. Then they put their hands on us and gave a blessing. Remember I said Olivia had electric hands?"

Sarah's head bowed her head down hiding a large grin.

Justin squirmed a bit and scratched his head. "Well, I've been feeling different on the inside since then. It's a peaceful kind of feeling. At first I thought it was just because I'm living with someone crazy about Jesus, but that's not really it. It's something else, but I can tell it's something joyful--something I haven't quite figured out yet."

Sarah cupped her husband's cheek. "You've been given a gift my dear, a very old, and precious one: the Holy Spirit."

"Oh go on!"

"I'm serious. Just don't turn away from this presence you feel. As time goes on, your doubts will be answered, and I'm very, *very* happy for you. That gift is even better than the one I'm giving you tomorrow."

"Uh Oh, Sarah, I'm really sorry. I didn't remember to get you any presents for tomorrow. It's Christmas, and I do know how important it is for you—and now for me too. Sorry."

Sarah chuckled. "Not to worry. I know you're just an amateur this year, and wrapped presents really aren't the important thing. Anyway, mine's just a small gift. However, I *do* have another present for you, a big one. But it's something you can't open."

Justin snuggled next to Sarah and gave her a little neck nibble. It made her chirp and giggle. "Well, guess what. I lied. I actually do have a big present for you too. And you can't open this one either."

CHRISTMAS

Sarah woke up in the dim early morning light and saw Justin leaning on the sill, staring out the bedroom window. She asked, “Honey, what were those awful noises that kept waking me up all night? Sounded like things flying overhead.”

Justin turned around with a grin. “Well, it wasn’t Santa’s sleigh.”

“Very funny.”

“They were aircars, dear. And they were deliberately avoiding the standard silent approach pattern. They wanted everyone to know they were coming down.”

“Who’s coming?”

Justin pressed a mark by the window and it glided open to one side. A rhythmic clump, clump noise filled the room. “Come over and see.”

Sarah shuffled over and put her arm on his shoulder. Down in the street, eight riot geared soldiers were jogging by in tight formation. Justin answered her unspoken question. “They’re all SD troops, lots of them. Show of force thing. I’ll call my Security Chief and find out if something has happened.”

He dressed quickly and picked up the living room vid phone. A message appeared: “Vid phone use is forbidden at this time.” He turned to Sarah with a puzzled frown.

She tied her robe, and kissed him. “Merry Christmas, darling. I’ll warm up some muffins and make coffee.”

“Well, I’m glad you’re taking this well.”

From the kitchen Sarah called back. “I know what it is. I remember Margo told me earlier. It’s just our power mad dictator having a temper tantrum.”

Doors closed and pots clunked. “He’s probably still furious about the failed Spero capture on word-wide television, not to mention that policeman refusing his orders to kill. Aten thinks these troops will scare us on Christmas, but it does look like we’re getting ready for a foreign invasion, doesn’t it?”

“Except there *is* no other Country to invade us.” Justin listened in amazement as his wife hummed a Christmas Carol. She swung into the living room with coffee mugs and a grin. "Well if I'm supposed to be in charge Sarah, I want you for my chief advisor."

Sarah put the mugs down, put a finger over her lips to remind him of the monitors, and whispered through a giggle: "I accept."

Both flinched when a loud repeating alarm suddenly blasted from the vid phone. "Urgent broadcast," Justin said. The device came on automatically and the radiant, golden sun logo of the Supreme Directorate appeared on the screen.

Attention citizens, this is a worldwide alert. We will be conducting exercises in every city today. Only personnel on the essential list will report to work. All others are required to remain in their homes.

The audio transmission paused. They looked at each other with raised eyebrows.

Should any citizen or group of citizens have governmental concerns, the proper procedure is to inform the city representative. Protests in the street are unsafe and illegal. They will continue to be met with appropriate action. Anyone who wishes to have a meeting of six or more persons will register with the police. If approved, they may hold the meeting in a designated public site.

(another pause) *Until further notice there is a curfew in effect after twenty one hundred hours. Anyone in the street after that time and before zero six hundred hours will be subject to arrest. Print function is active on your receivers for the next ten minutes. You will post this notice on the inside of your exit door. End of transmission.*

Justin chuckled. "Merry Christmas to you too, Aten."

Sarah was nodding her head. "Actually it's his feeble attempt to *steal* it. If you can't stop the holiday sick out, then own it. More than anything he wants to feel he's in control."

Justin pressed print. "I'm beginning to realize I'm married to a much wiser woman than I thought."

He picked up his coffee mug and walked over to the patio window. The view over the courtyard and into the hills beyond had taken on a different mood. A light dusting of snow had dressed the branches overnight. Its peaceful beauty gave him comfort. *I guess it's only the pine trees that stay green all year,* he mused. After a little while, he turned back to Sarah, and shrugged.

She shuffled over to him and whispered in his ear. "No opening presents until after breakfast."

Her lips tickled. Justin laughed and slipped his arm around her waist. "You're just not going to let Aten's tantrum get to you, are you?" She shook her head. "Well, whatever you're cooking it sure smells good in there."

# # #

They deliberately made small talk during breakfast should there be anyone listening. Afterward, Sarah went to the bedroom door, and leaned on the frame. She crooked her finger with an impish grin.

Once inside their "Christmas Sanctuary" she sat Justin down on the corner sofa chair. Then, she reached down behind it and produced a green envelope attached to a small present wrapped in red paper. "Open the card first."

"So, this how it's done, huh?"

She nodded and sat on the chair arm beside him. Her card was a hand drawn Christmas tree with a descending dove above it. Inside, she had carefully written: "Darling, may you always remember being so loved on our first family Christmas. Love Forever, Your Sarah"

Justin tilted his head up and for a moment their gaze locked. Emotion and tears overcame him. "And I *do* hope you know just how crazy much I love you too, Sarah." She gave a few quick nods, pulled his head closer and kissed his curly top hair.

Sarah wiped her eyes and said, "There's just one present to open 'cause I really didn't expect one from you this year. It's just a little something."

Inside the small box lay a medal with a silver chain. "You gave me a necklace?"

Sarah giggled. "No, it's an antique Saint Christopher medal. People used to wear it under their clothing, and it was supposed to protect you in your travels. Really it's just a reminder that those who love you are praying for your protection. On the back it says 'To Justin, love Sarah'."

"I love it dear. This is fun. Now tell me, what's the present I can't unwrap?"

Sarah slid off the chair arm, giggled, and leaned against the window frame. She cocked her head and gave him a sly smile. "It's actually a *future* present, something you gave me too in a way. Want to guess?"

After a moment his quizzical expression became a suspicious one. "You don't mean--but my arm implant was only taken out three months ago."

"Yes, and average men usually take over two months to become fertile. Apparently this doesn't apply to super heroes." Justin jumped up and they embraced in happy laughter and kisses. "Now, I know you didn't buy me anything Justy, but don't think I've forgotten you told me you had a surprise for me too."

Justin held her at arms length. "Oh, yes, yes. I almost forgot. Well, it's *kind* of a present, but you might not accept it since it's strictly illegal. Maybe I shouldn't have mentioned it." He paused for effect, happy that her expression remained puzzled.

"Justy, don't think for a second your not going to tell me."

He chuckled. "OK, you're aware that only Directors can call other cities, and only on business, right?"

Justin searched Sarah's face, but still found no sign of understanding. "OK, at ten o'clock tomorrow I've arranged for an encrypted call from our bug free room at the QDT. Anyone listening in will hear a recorded business call, but it will be decrypted at the other end. I've set up a call for you to South Africa. You'll be able to speak with your parents."

Sarah stood, hand over mouth in stunned disbelief. Her eyes slowly widened as comprehension grew, and she started jumping up and down. "My God! My Mom and Dad? It's been *seven* years." She embraced Justin and they both began bouncing together. “They don’t even know I’m *married* much less expecting.”

Tears came streaming down, and her head fell on his shoulder. “No one ever gets to even *write*, much less to talk to their family again. This is the greatest present ever.” Rapid kisses began. “Oh thank you, thank you, *thank* you.”

Laughing, Justin put his hand on her navel. “Hey, not too much of this jumping around, pregnant lady.”

THE CHALLENGE

"Welcome to the day after Christmas everyone, and the day after Aten's ultimatum." Paul settled them down with arm motions. "I want you all to understand, it's *perfectly* OK to change your mind. This is completely voluntary. No one is forcing you to be soldiers, but know that challenging their weapon will be considered an act of war."

A slight woman with short straight hair raised her hand. "But, the box shouldn't hurt us now, right?"

"Although we have all been immunized and Anna has checked us to the best of her ability, you all should realize there are no guarantees. It's never been tested with live people in the field. Also, even if their sound doesn't kill us it may still hurt, and in their anger the police might retaliate with force."

Paul studied the intense expressions. "Just because you volunteered to stand up to the SD weapon, there's no shame for anyone who wants to back out now. The troops could even open fire on us out of fear or frustration. This is a dangerous mission."

A chorus of "Let's go" and "Let's just do it," filled the break room. "Good. And so you all know, I'll be right up front. Remember there will also be over two hundred volunteers who will surround us on my signal, a not so subtle show of support. I've asked them to keep to a safer distance, a distance where there were no fatalities the last time they used the box."

# # #

By noon, resolute citizens were gathered in from all parts of Carolina Dome. Both average citizens and Humwa converged across the street from Chairman Margo's office building. Paul felt his pounding heart as he stood on the sidewalk next to them. *Looks like eight SD army police guarding the entrance. No local police and no sign of the black boxes yet, but they're paired up and fully* armed.

"All right, people, pick up your signs. The twelve of us will go up the steps as far as they will let us. Walk slowly and follow me. We are video recording this from the building behind us."

The group marched toward the building, but Paul stopped them at the foot of the steps. He went up two steps and turned to face them, perspiration now dripping from his face. He waited for their final nods of approval before he turned toward the entrance doors.

The SDs moved their rifles to the ready position. The glowing red lights on each weapon indicated that safeties were off. Paul realized he was trembling and the others sensed his fear. He was comforted when he felt his hands being gently grasped on either side. One was Singh, the other Ella, a black woman who worked in the City Accounting office. Deep throaty sounds began to resonate from Ella, and soon they were all singing "Amazing Grace" and slowly ascending the steps.

They reached the first landing and the Malthus statue before the guard Captain briskly strode down the steps to meet them and shouted "Halt!"

The menacing U-shaped entrance surrounded them, and every gun was pointed at them, but Paul felt a determined calmness wash over him. "We have a petition of demands for Aten with signatures from every city in the world. We request an immediate audience with the Chairman."

The Captain waved his rifle toward the distant throng. "And they are *all* with you as well?"

"Yes."

A military assistant hurriedly came out a side door wheeling a cart. He handed a black box to every pair of soldiers. The Captain held up a hand for Paul's group to wait while he conferred on his communicator. Then he said, "You twelve—are you the leaders of this uprising?"

Paul responded, "We are, but this is a simple request from the world's citizens, not an uprising."

Much to Paul's surprise the Captain holstered his communicator. "You have been granted a meeting, provided only that all those other people out there will remain quiet." Paul nodded, and spoke into his phone.

The Captain pointed to a soldier guarding a side door. "All of you: follow that man."

His sergeant led the twelve through the door and into an elevator that took them down to the basement level. *They are following some pre arranged plan,* Paul realized. *Must be a contingency for an action like ours. But what was it?*

They ushered the group into a spacious, white-walled interrogation room. The twelve took seats around a long, black granite table. The room had a one-way observation glass panel and multiple speakers recessed into the walls. When the sergeant left them, Paul said: "I'm sure you all understand that everything is being recorded. We are more likely under arrest at this moment rather than being allowed to talk."

The door slid open and the sergeant returned, pushing a cart laden with tea, cakes, grapes and dates. He turned around at the doorway before he left. "The Chairman sends you her regards. Someone will be with you shortly."

The team waited about fifteen minutes. Ella and two others had the courage to try the food. Ella shrugged. "Fresh and delicious. Try the little cakes."

Singh grinned. "At least we know poison isn't their weapon of choice."

Paul massaged his temples. *Yeah, but I just remembered. I think they do this before they sacrifice people to the Sun God.*

An announcement came over the speakers: "We are checking the sound system. Nod if you hear this clearly." A moment later a horrendous screeching blast caused some to fall to the floor. Everyone held their ears in agony. Later they would learn this was coincident with the same sound blast from the black boxes on the steps.

Recovery took awhile. Two women were crying and were afraid to unstop their ears. Others were less affected, but after several minutes, everyone was sipping the tea, waving and smiling at the one way mirror.

A few more minutes passed before the door opened once more. A tall, olive skinned man in an SD military uniform strode into the room carrying the latest assault weapon. "Sorry about the sound system malfunction," he sneered. "I am Aboud P666 from the Supreme Directorate. Your Chairman is not available at this time. The SD has assumed temporary charge of her office."

Paul grinned. "But actually Aboud, you're really sorry you didn't find twelve dead bodies in here, right?"

Aboud's sncer curled into a half smile. "Yes, well you people have surprised us once more." He nodded. "Personally I respect a worthy enemy. I see you had seven cities all timed to this same moment, and with the same protest. It appears that all your people continue to be uh--healthy."

Paul kept grinning. "We could have gone to twenty one cities, but it was short notice." Aboud's angry look flashed at him.

Paul raised his hands. "Aboud, perhaps you would care to just murder us all right now, the old fashioned way. We're unarmed, and you could use that old excuse, what was it? Oh yes, 'They were running away.'" Several in the group wheeled toward Paul, open mouthed and wide eyed.

They moaned as Aboud lifted his rifle up, flipped off the safety, and pointed the weapon at Paul. Then his snarl turned to a genuine smile, and he lowered the rifle. "Good fortune smiles on you people today. This decision is not up to me. May I have your, uh-- complaint list at this time."

Aboud snatched the paper as soon as Paul produced it. "I assume this is the same list that will be given at the other six cities?"

"It should be, but they are free to make additions."

The soldier activated something on his headset and spoke into the air. "You've seen this, sir. Instructions?"

Aboud slid the safety back on his rifle, and relaxed it on the carry strap. "I am authorized to tell you that a meeting to discuss your issues has been ordered to take place at the SD, next Wednesday at noon. Each Dome will send a *single* representative by Air Car departing at zero six hundred hours, SD time."

Paul said, "I, uh, sure." He looked around the room for nods. "That should be satisfactory for now."

"You must assure us there will be no more demonstrations until that meeting."

“Yes, agreed.”

“And how will you inform the other cities?”

Paul chuckled. “We have fast runners.”

Aboud was not amused. He snapped his boots together, stood at attention, and slapped his hand over his heart. ”Mercy of Aten.” He wheeled around and left.

Paul put a finger on his lips as he turned to the others. Their faces “shouted” both joy and disbelief.

WAITING

Paul worked in a top floor corner office at the QDT, and one side window provided a view of the Chairman's front steps a few blocks away. He would glance down during the day to keep watch and report on any gathering crowds, but all remained quiet since Justin's order. In fact, peace prevailed throughout the world while everyone waited for the results of the Supreme Directorate conference.

Paul was busy supervising two Departments in Justin's absence. With his back to the door, he was intent on his computer work when he heard a gentle knock. "Door's open. Come on in."

A soft voice came from behind him. "Uh, sorry to bother you, Paul. Do you have a minute?"

Paul spun around and was confronted by Sarah's large, worried eyes. The paleness of her face made her freckles stand out like tiny coffee stains on alabaster. "It's been three days now. I--just wonder if you--you have so many contacts. Have you heard anything--anything at all?"

Paul sprinted to her side and to give her a quick hug. He held her at arms length. "Oh, Sarah. Of *course* you're worried. But really, he's fine. I'm sure of it, but all I definitely know is the meeting is actually taking place somewhere in the SD complex. As you'd expect, they are keeping everything quite secret."

"I--I know. Justin would have called me by now if he could. I know that. Those people are so evil."

"And I know that too, Sarah. More than most."

"Oh God, *right*. They tried to kill you, didn't they?"

"Yeah, and some others around the Planet too, but now they know their big weapon is useless. They have no idea how we did it, and things have changed for us. Aten and the SD should be in fear of our numbers, our resolve, and the truth we stand for. They won't risk hurting Justin or the other representatives."

"So, you really think we have the upper hand?"

"Sure do. Wait 'til your husband gets back from the negotiations. I'll bet we'll finally have more control of our world."

Sarah touched her head. "Well, up here I know you're right." She patted her chest. "But, in here it's all acid and tight."

“Wait, didn’t you hear from Gretchen?”

“I’ve been out walking most of the day.”

“Well, she left you a message. We want you over for dinner tonight. Don’t you even *think* of saying no.”

“That’s really nice of you, but…”

“Sarah, really. You *have* to come. Lori and Tom from your God group are coming, and Gretchen really wants to see you. She’s been worrying about you and they want to pray for you. You shouldn’t be home all by yourself.”

Sarah threw up her arms. Tears streamed down her cheeks. “But see…” sniff, “I handle these things better when I’m alone.”

“That’s nonsense. Besides I have our network connection at my apartment. If you’re there, you’ll be the very first to know when Justin’s coming back.” He handed her a tissue.

Sarah wiped her cheeks and gently blew her nose. With a nod, she whispered, “Okay.”

# # #

Gretchen led a short prayer meeting after dinner, and Sarah told everyone about Justin’s new found belief. This was followed by a round of rejoicing and hugging. Lori reassured Sarah. "I know your love for him is off the charts dear, but don't worry. If God is with him now, he's under His protection. Remember, there's nothing that *He* cannot do."

After much encouragement and a little teasing, they finally got Sarah laughing. At last she confessed to being "blessedly assured", and she was able to finish dinner, her first full meal in days. She made eye contact with her hosts. "You know, I do want to tell all of you about--something exciting. We're secure here, right?" Paul nodded.

"Okay. Justin did the most wonderful thing for me before he--he left." She began to tear up. Gretchen walked over, put her arms around Sarah's shoulders, and kissed the top of her head. Sarah laughed and waved her away with the tissue. "I'm fine, really I am. Well, Justy arranged a secret call for me. I got to actually speak with my *parents*."

There was a chorus of yeas and Paul said, "And that's one of our negation requests, too. We want everyone to be able to call any city. Well, how are they, Sarah?"

"Mom's fine. She's still in her God Group, and they have a little secret place where she has a garden. But Dad's very sick, probably liver cancer. They wouldn't tell me more. But before that he was promoted to head of the

Graphene Chip Department, and they just had a wonderful vacation trip at the beach. I got to tell them about the years I spent getting to know his mom, Eula. They were so delighted."

Sarah did a little bounce-bounce on her chair. "But best of all I got to tell them I just got married, and how much we're in love." Giggles. "Mother said she remembered seeing him on video when he saved professor Main. Daddy remembers he actually met Justin on business once. Isn't that just great?"

Gretchen patted her hand and tried to make eye contact. "My intuition tells me our sweet young woman might have some other news too?"

Sarah's face squinched, and she rolled her doe eyes around the room. "How *does* this woman know things? Yes, I'm pregnant, too."

The ladies squealed, and took turns with their hugs and congratulations. Paul passed out a taste of Port from Pogo's. "This calls for a little celebration. And Sarah, you absolutely *must* stay in our guest room tonight."

She rose with a polite smile, "Thank you all for your concern, but I…" A loud buzzing came out of Paul's study.

He jumped up and everyone followed him into the room. “Encrypted message coming in.”

The screen read “Meeting over. There will be no world announcement coming out of the SD. Air cars are starting to depart at this time. Arrival times…” They waited patiently as different cities moved across the screen. Finally: “Carolina Dome, 0900 hours.”

After a little jumpy dance, Sarah told Gretchen, “OK, I guess I’ll accept your offer.”

Good. We have a quiet room with soothing sounds, and I’ll get you something to help you sleep.”

“Warm milk and honey? Do you really think I’ll sleep better with that?”

Gretchen hugged her. “You will, I promise. No one celebrates New Years Eve anymore. It will be quiet, but don’t worry, I’ll wake you at six.”

NEW YEARS DAY

The Air Car Arrival Center was packed with people and anticipation. The attendants made room through the crowd for Sarah, Paul and Gretchen when they came, but soldiers and police were nowhere in sight. Sarah's voice broke through the silence, the elbowing, and the perspiration. "So, Paul, there's no early word at all? Nothing about how the negotiations went?"

"Not a thing, Sarah. All we know is that the delegates from each city were put on Air Cars and sent home. The Chairmen and the delegates will make separate presentations in each of their Domes at the same moment worldwide. We're lucky we got a daylight time."

Sarah gave her hair a few quick pulls with a comb and smoothed her bright print dress. "So, basically we know nothing?"

"Yup. World Media's down as you know. Margo's people have set up a stage on their steps and patched in audio to all the big speakers in the street. We'll make a recording of our own, of course."

Sarah stood on tip toe. "It's almost nine now. Look, is that the car?"

Paul squinted toward the direction where she was pointing. "Up there? No, just a windblown cloud patch. He'll be coming in lower, over that rise to the right."

Sarah turned to Gretchen. "How do I look?"

"Like the prettiest woman in the world, dear." Gretchen turned her around and lightly massaged her shoulder. "Don't worry Sarah. I'm sure he'll be here any…" The crowd roared.

An air car flashed over the hill and slowed rapidly as it came closer. It floated over the trees and turned around. Sarah feared it might be changing its mind. But slowly, the car backed down over the landing pad, and descended with white jet puffs until it touched down.

A moment after landing, Justin swung out the door, briefcase in hand, and waving. He was the only one to disembark, and as soon as the entry port closed, the car roared off to another city.

Sarah bounced over to her husband to bestow hugs and kisses while others shouted questions. As Justin eased Sarah to the ground, Paul touched his arm. "Good news or bad, my friend?"

"Both I guess, but at least we are better off than before. The main thing is we've got a dialog going. Are we set up somewhere to make the announcement?"

"Yes. Ready when you are. Car's waiting."

# # #

Anna and Singh greeted them in the limousine, and she couldn't help but read some thoughts. They put a quizzical look on Anna's face. "Tell us all about the SD, Justin. We set your speech time for nine thirty but first we're taking you to a quiet place first for a short rest."

"Thanks. Well the SD's in a huge glass pyramid as you know. Almost no one gets in there except the Elect. Even Chairmen only get an inside audience once every five years. Our driver pointed out a stone building next to it where the city reps and Chairmen meet twice a year."

"Well, that's boring. So you only got to go into the Administration Building?"

"Not even. They had us meet in a small Agro Dome two hundred meters south of the compound. Our gathering was behind temporary barriers in some hydroponic field. We sat on metal folding chairs while six SD negotiators looked down on us from their stage. Troops were everywhere."

Sarah stroked Justin's hair. "So, no chance to hurl a spitball at the Great Aten, huh? Sounds like you were all treated like edible plants." She smoothed his early cheek stubble down with the back of her fingers. "This control thing is his consuming disease."

Justin slumped back into the soft car seat and closed his eyes. "Sorry guys, first moment I've had to relax." They let him close his eyes for awhile resting his head on Sarah's shoulder.

The car bumped to a stop and Justin's eyes snapped open. "Wait, I guess I should tell you all about the incident that happened when we were there. I won't mention it in my speech."

"Someone was hurt?"

"Yeah. It was on the second day. One of the agro workers I think--anyway it was some woman. She tried to scale the barrier around the meeting to get over to us. I only saw an arm and part of her face on top of the fence. She was screaming about wanting to go back with us. The poor woman was really hysterical."

Gretchen held her head. "Oh, no. They're mistreating the field workers, too. Doesn't surprise me."

"Yeah, but you had to feel sorry for her. I couldn't see much of the struggle, but it sounded like they stunned her in the end. Her screaming just stopped."

Sarah reached out for Gretchen and Justin's hands. "We have time. Let's pray for her."

"Oh, I just remembered, one guard shouted, 'You'll pay for this, Irene.'"

"All right, let's pray for Irene and the other workers."

# # #

Margo was waiting for them on the podium outside her office building wearing an indelible sneer. Justin made his way up the stairs with Sarah on his arm. Margo turned and murmured to him: "I won't have much to say on the behalf of the Directorate, but I will be the one to make the closing remarks."

The streets and the large square were packed with expectant faces. Justin took the microphone and gave them a big grin. "Have you heard this little forbidden tune?" He sang: "It's so good to be in Carolina in the morning." Applause and whistles.

"Well it is. It's great to be back." He paused and studied the crowd. "First off, if any of you have been hopping for a completely new government, I'm afraid you will be disappointed, or at least you'll have to wait. But for those of us yearning for a beginning of hope, peace, and dialog, I believe we've made progress."

Justin put both hands on the podium, his face becoming somber. "All the city representatives have returned from the Supreme Directorate with a signed agreement. There will be changes in our way of life through concessions from both sides."

Justin offered a faint smile. "Humwa will be pleased to learn that their pay will be raised to eighty percent of base and granted two weeks annual vacation. Also, Humwa may now vote, but will still not be allowed to hold office."

"Good news for music lovers and artists. Drawing and making music are no longer crimes. Public concerts and displays may be held as often as weekly, but live musical instruments remain banned. A music synthesizer will continue to be used, but it will be better quality since it will be played live. Of course, all content will be pre-screened to avoid anything they consider subversive to the state."

"Any meetings, and *even* God meetings, may be scheduled." He bent over as though he were confiding in the first row. "We had to really insist on that one. However, there'll be a presiding Centurion at all these meetings."

Justin coughed and took some water. "Getting approval for any kind of a God meeting was the most difficult, but they finally relented with one provision: the controlling administrator can stop it or interrupt it. I believe the phrase they used was 'for guidance'."

Justin was disappointed with the somber response of his audience. "Listen to this. For those of us who like good food, anything in short supply may now be filled by formerly Black Market items if they pass inspection."

The crowd remained silent. "I was hoping for more enthusiasm by this point since I'm almost out of the good stuff. We only got one change in the sixteen year old migration. They're really hard nosed on this one. But, from now on, should a young person enroll in police training, he or she may remain at home until they're eighteen." A few quiet boos wafted through the crowd.

Justin stood fully erect. "Sorry, but we are still unable to elect a Chairman." Margo snapped her head around with an ugly scowl.

"We were also unable to get permission for uncensored worship, or for stopping those annoying sunrise and sunset homage chimes. As you know, the SD considers these sacred." Louder boos.

"Look, look. I realize we didn't get much of what we wanted right off, but please think of this as a start in the right direction. Here's some really good news. The SD has pledged that no more people will disappear. They also promise no more unpunished police violence as long as we refrain from street demonstrations and sick-outs." Justin noted Margo was moving toward the podium. *She expects me to hand her the mike, but I'll finish when I'm ready.*

"In conclusion, I am asking you to just give this agreement a chance. The most important thing is this: we've started a dialogue. Remember that these are the first real changes we have seen in a hundred years, and we can hope for more in years to come." He held up a document. "This agreement may not be all that we want, but it does assure us of real peace."

Exhausted and frustrated, Justin looked up at the sky above the open dome. Circling above was the largest white bird he had ever seen. *An eagle?* He brought his attention back to the audience. "Copies will be made for everyone. I thank you for your patience and your trust in me." The people applauded politely.

Both Margo and Justin were startled by Sarah who demurely took the microphone from her husband, stepped down a few steps in front of the podium, and faced the people. With the resonant voice of authority she began: "God's blessings to all my brothers and sisters."

She turned as she spoke, drilling those in the front row with a penetrating stare. "It has been three hundred years since faithful Jews returned to Israel, and I have had a vision that this will be a year that heralds their peace as well as ours. But this peace will not come to you through those pieces of paper. My wish for all of you is a Happy, and mist importantly, a Holy New Year."

Margo had followed her down and grabbed the microphone. "What my former receptionist is trying to say is that peace will not come simply because we signed these papers. You must honor your agreement with Aten. Let us all look forward to this New World Order."

Margo returned to the dais and glowered at Sarah who moved in beside her. "Justin 126 has correctly presented the negotiated changes. The World Chairmen, myself included, have heard from Aten in person this morning in our chambers. He is pleased, and expects this agreement to end the unrest of his people. Aten regards these changes both as a Peace Treaty and his act of mercy."

Margo flipped the off switch on the microphone. She thumped it down, motioned for her people to end the broadcast, and walked away.

Sarah's face was serene. Her eyes glistened. Justin started to embrace her but she whispered. "Perhaps I should have just a few more words with our people."

His eyes grew wide, but he picked up the microphone and flipped the on switch. "Hold on one minute," he said to the dissipating crowd. "Hold on. My wife has something more to say to you."

At this, Margo's assistants ran to the control box at the side of the stage, but found Anna and Singh sitting on top of it, grinning and immovable. This was not the moment for a public fight.

Sarah looked toward the workers and the police who were grabbing wires and looking for something to unplug.

Margo was wildly signaling “cut”. “Don’t worry, Margo. I’m not going to speak against this agreement.”

She put her hands on the podium. “To all those who know the presence of our loving God, I ask that you do not reject the Centurions who will now be in attendance at our worship meetings. Remember, *all* are always welcome.”

Sarah’s face was radiant, and the throng stilled. “I have seen a vision. This year will end with our world in peace, but I see not only peace, I see freedom, and not only freedom but justice. I see redemption for all who follow Him, and I can see His love surrounding us.”

She glanced around at the entranced crowd. “There will yet be severe trials, but persevere. God wants all of you to know you will see His unfailing love in this year to come. May the indwelling of His Holy Presence reassure, guide, and strengthen every soul on our planet.”

The people all looked up. The great white wings had returned and hovered above them. “Behold, the angel of the Lord. He is heralding what is to come.”

The crowd raised their arms up and began to sway. “Nineteen hundred forty eight was the first new Jubilee.” Sarah raised her arms upward and shouted. “We have come to the year of the seventh Jubilee. Let us all rejoice.”

AFTERTHOUGHTS

A model of fundamental physics predicts there could be 10 to the $_{500}$ *power of different sets of laws when a universe (like the one we call home) is created. In our universe each of these laws seems precisely calibrated to the prerequisites for life.*

Discover Magazine, May 2009, p 51.

The combinations of physical laws that would have *prohibited* *the possibility of life far outnumber all the grains of sand on every beach on Earth.*

We may never find evidence for alternate universes. In ours, the cosmologic constant (necessary to support life) seems to be fine tuned to an exceptional degree.

Alejandro Jenkins & Gilad Perez, Scientific American, Jan. 2010, p 49.

ACKNOWLEDGEMENTS

I wish to thank the members of my writers critique group at San Diego Christian Writer's Guild, particularly our Temecula leader, Rebecca Farnbach. My thanks to all my proofreaders, particularly Fr. Don Kroeger at Christ Church, Fallbrook California. I send a special thank you to my mother whose advice was "Do what you enjoy, but just try and be good at it." The inspired cover painting was created by Connie Parkinson of Vista, CA.

Made in the USA
Columbia, SC
23 March 2022

57730021R00192